We're Only Human

So God keeps the Devil on his leash

By

Levende

We're Only Human

Scripture quotations are taken from the Catholic Bible Public Domain Version (CPDV)

Cover design by Oladimeji Alaka

With thanks to Chugalug & Ethaniel T

Dedicated to
P.J.T & O.T
&
Raymond Young: Author of (A Cure For The Nerves)

ISBN: 978-1-0369-0749-5

Email: levende@yahoo.com

Introduction

Many years ago, my brother, who had been going through many troubles in his life went missing. For ten agonising days, we waited anxiously for news of his whereabouts, not knowing if he was dead or alive. Not knowing can be the hardest thing, as your mind conjures up different scenarios with no conclusive answers.

There is a noticeable and tangible presence of evil within the world today, probably more so than ever before. With the uncontrollable advancement of technology and the devaluation of the individual human life, people are unaware of their unique importance in this continuous unfolding story. There is no longer the acknowledgement by many people that there may be the existence of a Divine Creator, the existence of God. We witness the destruction of the family unit all around us; and some people are no longer secure in their own bodies and crave more than their natural God-given perfection.

This escalating physical, emotional and drug fuelled 21st-century trauma is something that we witness every day before our very eyes. Destruction by our own hands and unaware or even worse, delight, and no thought for the consequences. We are so fearful of rejection from other people and yet do not give a second thought about rejecting the one who can save us.

This book of 32 stories reflects today's chaotic world and how, as a generation we are truly competent in one thing only: Slowly destroying ourselves and without even realising what is happening, until it is all too late.

As for my brother; he drowned.

Contents

The Kiss

Under the burnt red sun in the deadliest heat I was born.

A whisper was all I cried, for a scream was more than I could muster. My mother lovingly took me to her breast, but with tear-filled eyes for she knew it was all that she could do for me; but my mouth remained dry.

My only friend 'The Fly' who would look for death, would softly kiss me, yet I could find no strength to move him away from my skin. I would watch him, mesmerised by his dance which was occupying my mind and helping me to forget about my hunger and the pain that ravaged my fragile young body.

My sister; her belly swollen, and her eyes bulging from her head, would stare at me 'though lost of all expression'. She could not raise a smile, or at least until the day our parents laid her body into the dusty ground; then with a smile of relief upon her innocent face.

The fly returns to befriend her and kisses her on the lips. Our father buries her body with his torn and bloodied broken hands

Now I lay here, in this unforgiving deadly heat.
I thirst!
My body is struggling, fighting to live, but I know that I too will soon have a smile upon my face.

My mother's face;....... vacant!

My parents gave me the gift of life, and now the world is sending me to my death.

Now my corpse lies waiting; my soul has now left, but the fly still loves me and returns for one last kiss.

Luke 18:19-23

Then Jesus said to him: "Why do you call me good? No one is good except God alone. You know the commandments: You shall not kill. You shall not commit adultery. You shall not steal. You shall not give false testimony. Honor your father and mother." And he said, "I have kept all these this since my youth." And when Jesus heard this, he said to him: "One thing is still lacking for you. Sell all the things that you have, and give to the poor. And then you will have treasure in heaven. And come, follow me." When he heard this, he became sorrowful. For he was very rich.

Purity of love

The softness,
The freshness,
The true enlightenment of the purest love.

Without selfishness,
Without taking,
To love without asking to be loved.

The calmest, most peacefully perfect and purest gift of all is this.

Some emotions are without words to describe them.

The purity of love.

Matthew 22:36-38
"Teacher, which is the greatest commandment in the law?"
Jesus said to him, "You shall love the Lord your God from all your heart, and with all your soul, and with all your mind. This is the greatest and the first commandment."

Levende

To die in peace

As a group that started out as total strangers, we have become the closest of unlikely friends.

We sit in a dull lit room with only the faintest light. The dry and hot arid air scrapes our lungs and we can barely breathe. We talk very little because our minds are scrambled by the endless thoughts of nothing, and words have little or no meaning.

Week after week, and one by one, our friends are taken away by our captors. When the heavy wooden door opens, fresh air rushes in filling our lungs. Our hearts sink, and I hope they will not call my name; and when they choose one of our friends we sigh with relief, but with an overwhelming sadness because we know what is coming.

I desperately try to think of my family but cannot concentrate because my brain has crashed. I have no focus and cannot even begin to comprehend what is happening to us. I do not deserve this; none of us do. I do not want to die, not this way, not now! When I fall asleep, I dream of my home, of walking up to my house and my wife standing in the doorway to greet me. I remember the fragrance of my wife and our children.

Our children playing in the rain, splashing in puddles and the pure sound of innocent laughter. However, at some point my dreams have to finally end, and my reality returns.

Twenty-four hours feels like a lifetime, and a lifetime feels so far away, like an impossible dream.

Once more, the door opens, and we all look to the floor motionless in a childlike manner not wanting to be seen. Listening to their footsteps, they come over and stop. And without any sound, I feel a hand gently rest on my shoulder. Stunned by this touch my lungs deflate, and I finally surrender myself. I tremble uncontrollably as I get up to my feet. I look towards my friends, but they dare not look at me; their heads remain bowed, not wanting to allow the reality of what was happening to enter their heads.

For the first time since I have been held here, I am treated with dignity. They lead me to a room, whilst talking in a language I do not understand. As I enter the room, which is empty and has the stench of death, I look up towards the crumbling ceiling and at the blood-stained walls. In front of me I see a small window that is letting the light flood in, and there before me, I finally see the way I am going to meet my end.

Trembling and shaking in fear, I walk over to my executioner. My eyes full of tears blurring my vision, though I refuse to let one of them fall. I have been waiting for this moment for so long, now and all too soon it is here.
Oh Lord no! Save me from this.
Shackled, I kneel down, and I look up into their faces, knowing that they are the last people that I will ever see. I remember my

dreams; of my wife and our children playing in the puddles, and I think to myself, 'In less than 2 minutes, I will be released from this living hell, and I can return home.'

And there; there I see him, standing behind my captors, and then he speaks to me without saying a single word, and he pours an unimaginable calm into my aching soul. Then, in total serenity, I bow my head and close my eyes.

A single tear falls from my eye, though not in sadness nor fear, but in relief because now I know I will not die alone, and the last person that I will see with my mortal eyes is my Saviour.

I can go in peace.

Luke 2:29-30
"Now you may dismiss your servant in peace, O Lord according to your word. For my eyes have seen your salvation.

Levende

Path of life

As a child I learned how to stand. Then eventually without balance and with little or no control I started to walk.

I was on the move and no one was going to stop me. In fact, I could hardly stop myself.

The path that I was on, was level. It was like walking on a perfect polished marble floor.

I could go anywhere.

This newfound freedom was incredible, and I was in such a hurry, though not knowing where I was going; but I was off.

As I walked along, I noticed the path ahead eventually split into two separate directions. One level and wide, whilst the other slightly narrower with twists and turns.

I chose the narrow one.

The path that I had chosen, was at times overgrown with brambles and thorns, so I had to cut my way through, being careful not to stumble and fall along the way. It was no longer level and at times I had to push myself to carry on.

Whilst catching my breath, I looked out across as far as my eye could see, and I saw the other path. It was still level and was bustling with people, but it didn't appear to be heading in the same direction as where I wanted to go.

Even though by now I was tired, cut and blistered, I was not beaten. So again, and with a little more effort I carried on, though at times my life appeared to be full of confusion and no direction, like trying to complete a puzzle blindfolded.

Year by year, the four seasons continuously came and went. Aging me and wearing me out, weighing me down with pure exhaustion. Eventually, as I became an elderly man, I felt the path had almost completely disappeared, and I was now climbing the side of a mountain, struggling with every single breath I took.

Again, I looked across to the other path, which was still level and with many people laughing and enjoying a life that appeared to be full of pleasure.

I stopped and rested for a while before continuing. Whilst sat there, watching these other people, it made me question the choices that I had made throughout my life. I had to reassure myself that I was on the right path, even though I had been full of doubt so many times along the way.

By now every muscle in my old weary body was aching. I was struggling to get back up, but again I carried on.

Finally, when I reached the top of the path I had walked, stumbled and fell; I looked back at my journey and thought!

I remember thinking as a child that my life would be easy. I never realised that the path I had chosen would have been so difficult. Had I known what lay ahead, would I have set out at all?

Should I have chosen the easier path like the others?

But resting here now with my journey finally over, in a place that not even my wildest dreams could create, looking at all that I have seen and all that I have done. The hardships that life threw at me and trials that I endured have now disappeared from my memory.

I was on the right path, and I never strayed. Now, my journey is complete.

As for the others who took the level path, I wonder where they are now?

Hebrews 9:27-28
And in the same manner as it has been appointed for men to die one time, and after this, to be judged so also Christ was offered, one time, in order to empty the sins of so many. He shall appear a second time without sin, for those who await him, unto salvation

Levende

Prison

A modern minimalist glass penthouse rises up into the night sky, looking down at a city that never sleeps.

Modern minimalist people within its multi million-dollar walls relaxing and abusing a life full of luxury, with champagne and 'cocaine' lined tables; and as for money, if it were a liquid, it would flow from the taps.

A man sits alone on the balcony looking down at the city below, while his 'friends' indulge and abuse his good fortune.
He can see people below in the city streets like worker ants, hurrying around with no purpose that he can see; his self-importance is so much greater than their meaningless existence.

He then looks at himself, his material life full, but his soul completely empty of all humility. He sits and gazes out into the crisp city air, wondering, without knowing what to think.

Then, a single feather drifts down upon a breeze and settles into his hand. He takes the feather and stares at it for a while with a vague smile on his face. He then stands up, climbs onto the balcony, and balances on the stainless steel rail.

In his cocaine-filled mind, he wonders to himself, 'What would it be like to be a bird, to fly, to be free.'

He holds out his arms and tosses the feather back into the fresh evening breeze. As he launches the feather into the night sky, he slips on the rail and loses his balance. With all his might and child-like fright in his eyes, he desperately reaches out for safety, but;…….

The feather drifts aimlessly across the city until it finally floats down through a prison cell window.

A man is lying down naked on a cold stone floor, looking up at a blank concrete ceiling. This man is stripped of all that belongs to him, no clothes, no possessions, not even his dignity, but still a faith that lies deep within him. The feather continues to drift down and settles into his hand. He sits up, his eyes gleaming with delight, for this single feather is contact with the outside world that he no longer knows, a world that has forgotten all about him.

He lays back down with the feather in his hand, the only possession that he now owns, enjoying his good fortune. Whilst outside, he can hear a commotion and he watches blue flashing lights bouncing off his ceiling.

In peace, he closes his eyes and goes to sleep.

Psalm 142:6

I cried out to you, O Lord, I said: You are my hope, my portion in the land of the living.

Jerusalem

Lying wounded and dying in the middle of the city street that I have walked a thousand times, I watch my blood trickling past me whilst feeling my life slowly but surely ebb away. In pain, I pray for another breath and another, each one filling me with relief because I am still here; but also filling me with fear, for it may be my last.

Looking up, my family surround me, screaming and shouting, whilst drones swarm overhead. My vision is blurred as I drift in and out of awareness. My family's screams are now full of words that I cannot comprehend, and I can no longer summon my body to live. In the chaos, my mind starts to wander off to when I was a child.

I vividly remember looking out of my living room window, at the clouds that would slowly pass over our Senonian limestone city. I always wanted to jump up and catch the clouds in my hand, convinced that it was possible to bounce upon them.

There I would sit, lost in my imagination. I would sometimes look across to another window, in another apartment block, and see another boy with the same toys as myself. He would also look up at the same sky over the city that was 'ours.'

As I became older, I remember my friends and I would walk to school. The boy and I would pass each other every day, never talking but knowing who the other one was.

When we were teenagers, our different groups of friends would fight through nothing more than hatred inherited through our families' religious bigotry, but as for the two of us, we would never fight each other.

As I grew up and slowly became a young man, I could see our perfect city being torn apart for the sake of faith.

One day as I was walking home, a blast ripped through the street ahead. I ran, not knowing where to run, towards my family I hoped, then I saw him, the man I had known since we were children, running in the same direction. Another blast shook the ground beneath our feet, and he stumbled and fell to his knees. I stopped and ran back to help him to his feet. We continued to run side by side, but in the confusion and devastation, we went our separate ways.

Now a parent myself, I would sit and watch my son play by the same window, reminding me of my youth before my ears had ever heard the noise of destruction and the sound of death.

Today, for the first time, I was late for work, and I hurriedly said goodbye to my wife and son, rushed out of the door, and ran for the bus. As I approached the bus stop, I was caught in a blast, thrown through the air, and slammed into the ground by the

Devil's wrecking ball. This man, the boy I once knew, ran towards me; he bent down and cradled me in his arms without saying a single word, trying to stop the blood pouring freely from my body. We looked at each other as if we were the closest of friends. I have known this man for longer than any of my friends, yet I do not know him at all; we have never even spoken.

My family arrived, and in anger and shock, they chased him away. I stared at him as he staggered off; he then stalled, turned around and looked back at me as if to say goodbye. With his blood-soaked hands consoling his face, he turned and then walked away.

A soldier shouted to him, "STOP," but in his grief he continued walking until a single shot rang out and brought him to his knees; he slammed down into the ground with the dust rising to take him away from my sight for one last time, like a final curtain call.

I now lay here remembering my childhood, whilst my family scream and shout, my mother on her knees screaming to God with her arms stretched out looking to the sky, until their voices start to fade. Eventually, all I see are their mouths raging with despair and chaos everywhere.

I am so frightened.

'My son, my son, where is my son?'

My heart is the only sound that I can hear inside my thumping head.

As hard as I try, and with all the strength I possess, and against my will....

I close my eyes.

Luke 23:28

But Jesus, turning to them, said: "Daughters of Jerusalem, do not weep over me. Instead, weep over yourselves and over your children.

God's Cathedral

Along a country path I wondered.

Looking towards the ground, I saw the reflection of the sun dancing on the path. Moving and swaying in time with the leaves on the trees and everything was in rhythm with the breeze all around.

As I looked up towards the trees leading to the blue sky above, they were like solid columns, supporting the green and golden vaulted leaf roof that enclosed me, only for the break in the leaves where the sun pierced through.

The rustle of the wind rushing through was like a choir of angels singing from heaven above. It was then that I realised I was not on a path at all, but I was in a cathedral.

A cathedral as we know it, is built out of stone and by the hand of man. It is not alive but lives through the people within its walls and God's love.

The Cathedral that I was in was not built by man but raised by God and this Cathedral was alive in itself, through the columns of trees along with the leaves that support its roof, and the sun that every day continually lights our way.

A living breathing Cathedral created by God for us.

Sirach (Ecclesiasticus) 42:16
The sun illuminates and considers all things, and its work shows the fullness of the glory of the Lord.

Apartment 2820

Tonight, in the bitter and painfully freezing cold, I reached the depressing drab grey apartment block that I call home. I looked up towards the windows and noticed all the lights were on. My heart slumped, and I thought, 'I hope it's going to be a peaceful night.'

As I walked through the darkened lobby, one of the tenants was sitting on the stairs rocking backwards and forwards mumbling to himself, saying, "My Daddy dropped dead from a heart attack, Mommy got high on Cocaine, my sister fell in love with a noose on a rope, and I'm trying not to go insane."

I cautiously squeezed by him and climbed the dimly lit stairs because they are safer than taking the elevator. As I reached the 3rd floor, I could hear every sound that came from each apartment as I went by.

The music, the shouting, laughter, crying, orgasmic sex; the silence and finally, the family that lives in apartment 2820.

What I didn't know, and what I often wondered, was:

'What was actually happening behind each door? How different were the lives of the people that lived there? If I could actually see through walls, what would I see?'

'And would I really want to know?'

Apartment 2815

Lorenzo, A man I hardly know, a man I don't really want to know; was sitting around a poker table with his friends. With six half-full glasses and a bottle of tequila and smoke that filled the air, they took turns playing a game of chance with a revolver against their heads. With six chambers within the cylinder and a bullet which they had all kissed for their sick pleasure, the probability of a healthy outcome was not looking good.

Apartment 2816

Susan is a nurse, she kindly helped me once when I fell down a step outside. She is a woman with such a warm caring smile, which radiates compassion and humility. But what nobody realised was the fact that Susan was fighting her own demons, which she had hidden behind her smile for years, acting out a life that was not really her's, believing that no man could ever love her. Tonight after a meal and a glass of her favourite wine, she decided that she was going to vacate this life that has tormented her for so many years. Her plan is made, no further action is required, and in complete silence, she passes from our lives unnoticed.

Apartment 2817

Mason, a man I know little about! He has lived alone for the past three years since his girlfriend left him. I sometimes see him and Susan struggle to have a conversation in the corridor. They look at each other, waiting for the other to make the first move. I wish he would ask her, but he doesn't know what to say. He now lays in his bed, completely stoned, as the world drifts by without him.

Apartment 2818

Zayn and Emily live quietly here. They don't appear to work, but they don't seem to be broke either. They have friends visit all the time, and you can hear music from under their door; though behind the door is a very different story. A small film studio in an apartment that looks more like a penthouse suite from Beverly Hills. Two girls and a man naked, playing to the camera, fulfilling the pleasures of the people who watch them online, making money for fun.

Apartment 2819

Ben is an accountant, or at least he was; all he appears to do now is drink. In the past, I have had to step over and around him to get through my front door, with the stench of urine running from his legs drenching the floor, completely unaware of his surroundings. I wish I could help him, but I too am an alcoholic who has not had a drink for 15 years. Tonight, I can hear him singing the same songs as he always does whilst drinking a glass of Golden Guilt, before he once again argues with the man in the mirror and begins to cry, but I suppose to him, it all makes sense

Apartment 2820

Matthew lives here with his young family. He always says hello regardless of how late he is for work. He will knock on my door if he has not seen me for a few days, to ensure I am okay. Tonight, he tucks his children into bed and tells them a story, giving them a quick tickle so he can see the smiles on their faces, which gives him all the pleasure he needs. He then helps them to say their prayers before kissing them good night, and then he walks away content with his life.

Finally, I reach my front door and turn the key; and then hear a single gunshot come from apartment 2815.

I guess that didn't end well!
It's going to be another long sleepless night.

Matthew 28:20
Teaching them to observe all that I have commanded you. And behold, l am with you always, even to the consummation of the age.

Paradise

Standing on top of the highest hill, with the clearest bluest sky above.
I look down towards a vast valley below.

I close my eyes.

I see the glow of the warm spring sun piercing through my eyelids.
A pure breeze rushes towards me without coldness, filling my lungs.
Breathe in; breathe out, filling my lungs more than ever before.

I feel like new.

I look all around, taking everything in: blades of grass thick like a carpet, flowers like I have never seen before and colours that have no name.

This place feels so   'Perfect'.

I start walking down towards a city I can see towards the bottom of the valley.

I pass a trickling stream and stop to quench my thirst.
The water is so clear, and it is the purest, coldest water that I have ever tasted.

I rest for a while.

A bird flies down and lands beside me and starts to sing.
The calmest music that I have ever heard.
I place my hand out to the bird, knowing he should fly away in fear.
But no; instead, he rests softly upon my hand.

I start to walk on with not a thought in my head, yet full of clarity.
I am so complete.

I notice a gardener tending to his flowers, cutting back and pruning; he looks up raises his hand and smiles at me.

Where am I?

As I reach the bottom of the valley, I draw close to a city that has captivated me along the way.
A magnificent, brilliant white city that draws me ever closer.

I think to myself,

'If I were to die, this is what I would want Heaven to be like.'

As I approach the gates, there are people standing outside.
As I get closer, I recognise them.

My parents, my brothers and my sisters.
This cannot be true because they have all died, and now, here, they live.
My parents; younger than me, and I'm an old man.

I look up to them, thinking I'm dreaming, but they are real.

I hold my arms out to greet them and there I see; my tired old skin is new again.

I look, I feel, I am.

Luke 23:42-43

And he said to Jesus, "Lord, remember me when you come into your kingdom."
And Jesus said to him, "Amen I say to you, this day you shall be with me in Paradise."

Levende

Give me a chance

At first, I feel nothing but warmth.
I like this feeling.

I am conscious and aware, but of what?
I do not know.
The soothing dull drum that constantly beats comforts me whilst I sleep.
I know nothing; but my world is so peacefully perfect.

Slowly, new things come into my world.

Yesterday, I could see. It was   brightness!

It took my darkness away for the first time, but only briefly, like a warm golden-red glow; but it then disappeared again.

Now, something amazing happened.

It was "Happiness." Someone was happy. I heard it in my head—lots of happiness—it came from the sound that is connected to me. It wasn't me, but it was my world.

It was soft, beautiful and……nice.

I desperately want to be where the happiness is. I want to be happy with them. I want to see the soft voice that is part of me, I want to see the brightness, and for it never to disappear, I want to stay warm, wrapped in the love of the happiness and to feel complete.

When I'm not sleeping, the soft, playful sounds that I hear are constant, and one of them sounds like……"Mummy."

I'm going to call my world "Mummy." I like that! and it sounds ……..good.

"Mummy."

The sound connected to me is not happy; I do not like this new sound.

I feel something new, and it is not happy; I feel……………Sad.

"What is wrong sound?

Be happy."

It is now continuously sad.
I cannot be happy in my mummy if the sound is sad.

Oh no, I don't feel very well; I am choking, I am hurting, I am too young to feel pain, but I do.

Get it away from me; You do not belong in here; you're hurting me.

Get out!

Something has got into my mummy, and I cannot get it out; it's hurting.

If I had tears I would cry,

"Sound that is connected to me,…..Help me please!"
Something is wrong.
The sound is crying, and she cannot hear me.
I cannot survive!
Help me, please!

I need the sound to hear me.

I need to give the sound a name: think,………………………..…
think,……….……think.

"MUMMY."
"look after me, protect me, stop the pain; take it away,
"Mummy."

The golden-red glow is fading away.
Mummy, I need you; I love you; please help me.

Scream!

"MuMMY"

"Please help me, I hurt".

"Please."

"Mummy, Mummy, Mummy,..............Look Mummy, I can cry! Mummy, Mummy, Mu"......................................

Exodus 20:13
The Fifth Commandment
Do not commit murder.

Flatpack faith

Early on Sunday morning, when I believed I had earned the right to stay in bed, my wife in all her wisdom, decided that 'We' as a 'couple' should spend some quality time together.

"Okay!" I said with a degree of hesitation because this could only end in one way……disaster!

I asked her, "What would you like to do?"

"I was thinking about shopping" she replied.

"Ha, you have absolutely no chance" was my reply. That's put an end to that idea, and I turned back over.

Anyway, not too long after this, I found myself in our car and off on a hugely expensive shopping adventure.

We finally arrived at a colossal building which obviously had to have been designed by a woman because no man with any integrity or self-respect would put another man through what I was about to experience.

I could feel the frustration build up inside me, along with anger mixed with anxiety and dread because I knew that she would want to walk the entire length of this money-grabbing, relationship-destroying international tax looping empire, which proclaims that they want to make shopping with them a "Brand new experience."

Staying in bed would have been a wonderful experience and one that would have been free. Apart from that, I also knew that she would want to look at every single product for sale that has no relevance to our lives, plus she would try to explain why every item would be of great benefit to us. I knew I would have to show some vague interest, and to top it off; there wasn't even a TV department.

However, to my utter surprise, she did know exactly what she was looking for; unfortunately, I didn't! When she picked out a flat-pack dining table, I dumbly thought, 'Who's going to put that together?'

Two hours later, and back home, I found myself sitting on my living room floor with a screwdriver set that I unfortunately remember receiving one year for Christmas. I looked at the instructions and thought, does she honestly expect me to read this, try and understand something that makes no sense and build a 'table' that we really don't need?

I have been well and truly scammed!

Now feeling irate, I shouted very quietly so as not to be heard,
"No, No, No, I am not putting up with this nonsense, especially on my Sunday afternoon." Anyway, after getting cross and by this time putting my foot firmly down, I started to build this useless thing that was not going to 'enhance' our lives as she so ridiculously claimed.

After some considerable time, with blood tears and sweat, along with two cups of coffee, she came to see how I was getting on, and it was clear that I wasn't. She wore that patronising smile of "Oh dear" in capital letters all over her smug face.

She asked, "Would you like any help?"

"No," I firmly replied.

Then she said, "We could do this together, it would be an achievement."

"Fine," I replied in secret relief.

After several agonising hours, we somehow finished the table. As happy as I was with this small back aching credit to my name, I was still puzzled as to why we bought it in the first place.

"Come on" she said, "Help me get it into the car,"

Has this woman completely lost her mind? I could not believe what she was saying to me.

So, in total bewilderment and lost for words, we unscrewed the legs, put this marriage breaker into the car and left home. She drove for a while until eventually we came to a grubby little house with a front lawn that resembled a battlefield and a smashed-up car that had not been touched in years.

My wife rang the doorbell and a woman appeared and kissed my wife on the cheek. Two little children came running outside screaming with excitement shouting, "It's here, it's here."

The woman came towards me, gave me a hug, and said, "Thank you so much for your kindness."

"Ahhhh, it's nothing," was my stunned reply, not entirely understanding what was going on.

My wife came to my rescue by saying, "Let's get this table inside."

As I entered the house, I was greeted by a man in a wheelchair. I raised my hand to greet him, but I quickly realised that he was not able to do the same. Embarrassed by what I had just done, I followed everyone into the living room and there before me was a young boy also in a wheelchair.

In that single moment, I felt the ground fall away from under my feet, and my whole day flashed before me with the realisation of what today had been about.

Stunned and emotionally winded, I quietly put the table together. My wife and her friend laid the table and we all sat around for something to eat.

As I was about to pick up my fork, the man said a prayer for everything they had received. Shamefully, I could feel tears well up in my eyes ......

Galatians 2:20
I live; yet now, it is not I, but truly Christ, who lives in me. And though I live now in the flesh, I live in the faith of the Son of God, who loved me and who delivered himself for me

River of life

Early on a cold and crisp spring morning; a tiny raindrop fell from the sky.

It hurtled towards the earth and with a thunderous splash, entered a mountain stream teeming with life.

Then, unnoticed in a quiet tranquil calm, it slowly trickled down the stream, basking in the sun. The stream became faster and wider until, without knowing or realising, it had become part of the flowing river.

However, the raindrop was still a raindrop, but now indistinguishable from the other raindrops around it. The river was swelling, moving around in every possible direction, twisting and turning, crashing and rebounding like rush hour in Times Square on '*Speed*,' but with no time at all for the raindrop to see what was happening around it, completely lost in the mayhem. Taken on a rollercoaster journey over which it had little if no control.

More rain continuously crashes down, filling the river with new life, and the river's edge now disappears into the distance.

Now, as quickly as it fell into the stream, the raindrop was now leaving the river behind. The land that once encased the river was gone from sight and the blue sky above opening up and the water around now so vast. A torrent of crushing water pulled the raindrop under the surface.

The river has run its course and beyond this point, the journey must finally come to its end.

Gone!....

But instead of the journey's end, the raindrop finds itself in a new vastness teeming with life.

The ocean now marks the start of a new life; a new beginning.

2 Corinthians 6-8

Therefore, we are ever confident, knowing that, while we are in the body, we are on a pilgrimage in the Lord. For we walk by means of faith, and not by sight. So we are confident, and we have the good will to be on a pilgrimage in the body, so as to be present to the Lord.

The Mist

So, university had finally finished, and we were free. The hardest four years of my life were now completed. My cousin 'Alfie' and I were going to go travelling before life gets its grip on us, and this was something that we would never be able to do again.

We decided on the Far East. Mostly because our grandfather lived there for three years, some fifty years ago. He always compared everything here to his time over there, though we did often tell him that things had changed; that the world had changed since then.

He agreed with us, but pointed out this one small town which he never forgot; and how it was probably the closest place to paradise that he had ever visited.

We set off, and our first stop was the capital city that you would have thought stepped out of a 24th century comic book.

The city was immense and overwhelmingly busy. We noticed people would look at us whilst scurrying around, but oddly, no one would smile which made us feel uneasy, and not particularly welcome.

We booked in to our hotel, and were asked to complete a 'Visitor Information Request Form' (VIRF). I asked, why was this necessary, and I was informed that it was for our own safety. We completed the form and checked in.

After a few weeks we made a plan to travel towards the town that our grandfather often spoke about.

After some searching we finally found a place to stay. A hostel, which was close to the town. We arrived and after completing the necessary forms we then settled in, and then asked for directions to the town. The following morning we decided to go out and explore. Whilst walking about we noticed people again did not want to make eye contact, but we were aware that everyone was looking at us. We had some old photos which grandad took, so we decided to do 'Then' and 'Now' shots to take home for him.

We located some of the streets that he told us about, but most of the houses were abandoned, and being reclaimed by nature. We thought that we would go to the school, but that too had clearly been closed for years.

We found a temple, but again, no one. Finally we came across a small church. As we walked up the steps it was clear to see that the roof had caved in many years ago and the stained glass windows were almost completely gone.

As we walked up to the entrance, an elderly lady was sweeping the floor within the church, whilst singing to herself, and there was a vase of flowers where the alter once stood. She looked up, smiled and then continued to sweep.

We walked up to her and said, "This church must have been amazing when it was in use."

She looked up and replied, "Yes."

I asked her, "Do you sweep the floor every day?"

She said, "Yes."

I asked another question, "Do you live close to here?"

Again she said, "Yes," with a smile.

We thought, she has absolutely no idea what we're talking about. So Alfie said, "It was nice talking to you."

She said,………… "Yes."

We turned around and started to walk out of the entrance where the doors would have once stood, and we could hear her continuing to sweep.

I turned around and said, "I know you don't understand me, but I don't understand why you keep sweeping the floor, because the leaves will only come back in. It's pointless."

We started to walk away and she said, "I do this because this is God's house, and no one else is here to help me."

She understands!

With huge smiles we turned around and said, "You understand us."

She replied, "Of course, why wouldn't I understand you?"

"We thought, because you did not reply to us, you had no idea what we were talking about."

"I understand everything perfectly well, but many years ago my father taught me that it is wise to sometimes say very little, because you do not know who you are talking to."

"Your father was a very wise man."

She replied, "Yes." Though this time with a warm smile.

She then asked, "Why are you here? there is nothing to see; all the tourists stopped coming here over 30 years ago."

Alfie said, "Our grandfather lived here 50 years ago whilst in your country. We have just finished university and wanted to see where he lived, because he told us it was like paradise."

She smiled, "Your grandfather is right. It was."

I said, "Can I show you the photos that we have?"

"Yes please, that would be delightful."

I took out the copies that I had, and showed her. Her eyes lit up, but then as I watched her face I could see a sadness fill her eyes. I thought, this was a bad idea, and I said, "I am sorry I didn't want to upset you."

She put her hand on my arm and said, "Its nice to see these, its just upsetting to see how life has changed. This was a busy town when I was much younger; shops, and people working, and the smell of the food whilst you would walk by each property. Now, nothing. There are 38 people left, and the youngest is 65 years old.

People were given empty promises of better jobs in the cities, so they left in droves. And because they left, the school closed down, and because the school closed, the shops couldn't survive. Now, nothing. My neighbour was 87 last March, and we found her dead in bed. We had to bury her. The youngest of us, '65'. We had to dig her grave because all the young people moved to the 'City of Depression'. No one is happy there, No one! The promise of a better future, means, forget God, forget your family, and to forget yourself. And I tell you, the only thing to leave villages and towns like this are The shadows of the peoples former selves because your heart dies."

We didn't know what to say; 'Sorry" didn't seem to be appropriate.

With tears in her eyes she said "Come on, let me see the rest of your photos."

I carried on showing her the photos that we had, until we came to the last photo which was of our grandfather. She gazed at it for a while, then tapped it with her hand and said that he appeared to be a lovely man.

She then said, "My name is Agnes. Come to my home, it's time for some tea."

We spent the afternoon together. She told us about her life, and she was very interested in our family. At the end of the day we asked if we could take a selfie with her and then we thanked her for a special day.

Before we left, she said, "Whilst you are travelling, go to the monastery in the hills. I have not been there for years, but it is a very holy place."

We promised we would, and we said our goodbyes.

For the next couple of weeks we travelled around, met people and visited the usual tourist sites. Then Alfie said that we should go to the monastery. "We promised Agnes, and I think we should respect that."

We made our travel arrangements and set off the following day.

When Agnes said it was in the hills, she wasn't wrong. We arrived at the bottom car park, and looked up into the clouds, with no sign of a monastery. We decided to walk up, and so prepared ourselves for the trek, and set off.

A man called out, "Where are you going?"

"To the monastery!" I replied.
Everyone in the carpark laughed. 'Okay' I thought to myself, this is obviously a bad idea.

We set off and started to walk up a steep wide path, getting wet from the heavy mist that filled the air. After an hour, we heard the sound of a tractor coming up the hill. The driver stopped beside us. He was one of the men who earlier had been laughing.

"Get on trailer, me going to top."

With absolutely no hesitation, we climbed up and sat down next to some other people in the trailer, who were obviously more intelligent than us.

Alfie said to the driver, "How long will it take to get to the top?"

In broken English he replied, "40 minute."

As we ascended to the top, the mist started to clear, and we could see the green foliage and trees, and our clothes started to dry out.

The driver called out, "Look, look, see."

Eventually, we looked up, and the was this old magnificent building that you would only see in a story book. It rose up from the cliff edge, up and up as far as the eye could see. I couldn't believe my eyes.

We drove into a courtyard, and were asked to get off the trailer. All we could do, was stand there in amazement, mouths open, trying to comprehend what we were seeing.

Eventually we were ushered in to the hall, and were greeted by a monk. "Thank you for coming, and you are very welcome. Come, come."

I said, "There are not many visitors here today."

"No" replied the monk. "We do not get so many anymore. It is a big treck to get here, and unfortunately people think we're nothing more than a theme park. We may get a few people come on retreat, but society has done a very good job of convincing people that the only God they need is themselves or their phones!"

We followed him into a large room with a carved wooden beamed ceiling and were given some tea, and then shown around.

After looking around this incredible old building, we were taken into the chapel overlooking the valley. To the side, there was a large circular window, which must have been 20ft in diameter, and it was filled with stained and clear glass, so you could just about see outside. The large vaulted ceiling was blackened with the burning candles, of which there must have ben 300.

I asked, "Why do you have so many candles lit?"

He replied, "They are prayer requests which people have asked us to light."

"And why did you repair the stain glass window with clear glass?"

He said, "It is not repaired. Heaven shows us glimpses of what it is like. The window reflects this by showing glimpses of the natural world outside. If you look closely through the window, you can see the mist, acting like a vail between here and the outside world."

The monk then said, "Sit down and I will leave you here for a while. Try talking to God!"

He walked out, and Alfie and I just looked at each other, trying not to laugh.
I whispered, "Alfie, Alfie, how do you talk to God?"

He shrugged his shoulders, trying not to laugh, and said, "I don't know?   Hello?………..Is it me you're looking for!"

We both started to uncontrollably giggle like children, and then the monk walked in.

We tried to look serious, as we wanted to show respect for him.

I asked him, "How long have you been here?"

"17 years. I came here when I was 19."

Then big mouth Alfie said, "Why, why would you give up everything for this; don't get me wrong, it's a nice place you've got here, but 17 years, seriously! Why?"

He smiled and said, Alfie, you're right 17 years is a long time, but I gave up something to gain everything, and you can only understand this, when you understand!"

Alfie replied, "You're right, I don't understand."

He then said, "Alfie; "What is the world offering you? What desires of yours, does life fulfil. Money? Big house? Car? Women? What? because Alfie, I truly do not understand. Families are torn apart, people living alone in rented one bedroom apartments because they cannot afford to buy, and do not even know their neighbours. They're living in a twenty four hour virtual reality hologram. Masturbation, not procreation, fewer children are born, suicide is on the rise along with unemployment and the isolation of the elderly. Is this the sign of a progressive society Alfie? Is it? Tell me. People say, that this is my truth, or that is not my truth, or your truth is not my truth, or my truth is personal to me. Truth, truth, truth! What about a singularity perspective of factual truth. What about Gods truth? Everyone cannot be right, because then nobody can be wrong!"

Alfie replied, "I really don't know."

"No, but God does Alfie. He knows your heart, he knows you, but he will not enter if you won't let him in. And he's not called Lionel Richie."

I said, "You were listening to us!" The monk laughed and said "God loves laughter. Now come on, the day is getting late and it's raining, so we need to get you back home."

As we reached the courtyard, the driver of the tractor approached the monk and spoke to him. The monk came back to us and said that the rain was now far too heavy, and it was not safe to take the tractor back down. They told everyone that they would prepare some guest rooms for the night.

We were taken into a lounge, and given some tea. Then we were informed that it was approaching prayer time. During this time we could join them for evening prayer, or stay in the lounge.

I asked for the Visitor Information Request Form. The monk looked at us, then said, "Father Gregory, do you have the visitor request form?"

This short stocky man looked up and replied, "The What?"

The monk again with a smile said, "The visitor request form, do you have it?"

Father Gregory scratched his head and said, "I think I used it to light the fire a while ago. Why, who wants it?"
"Alfie does" said the monk.
Father Gregory came over to Alfie and said, 'Alfie, Alfie, God knows where you are, so the Government doesn't need too. It says 'Request' on the top of the form; well we are respectfully declining their 'Request'. God knows where you are, and that is all that matters. Now; are you coming for evening prayer? You are invited. That, Alfie, is a request."

I was intrigued, and as for Alfie; less so. "Come on Alfie, let's go down, we'll never get another opportunity like this."
"Why, to hear some monks 'Chant!'. Why would you want to?"
"Because we are here, thats why, and they are giving us a bed for the night, come on Alfie, let's go."

We entered the chapel once again, and along with the other guests' we sat at the back. Now with the evening falling in; and the rain hammering and pelting down, smashing against the stain glass window, the monks came in, in a prayerful contemplative silence.

As their prayers began, I felt peace, for the first time in a very long time. I looked towards Alfie; his jaw was dropped, just staring, captivated by what was happening. I don't think any of his senses were prepared for this; but then, I too was in awe by what was happening.

Alfie tapped me on the knee and whispered, "Serenity. This is complete serenity, I cant believe what I'm seeing."
Once the prayers had finished we headed back to the lounge where some supper had been prepared for us. After talking to the other guests for an hour, we decided it was time for bed. The following morning we got up, and gathered out belongings

We walked back to the courtyard, and to the tractor. The monk said that he hoped we had a peaceful time. Alfie said to him, "I don't think I am ready to leave."
The monk replied, Alfie, it's a nice place we have here; but do really want to stay another day. Seriously! Why?"
We laughed.
He smiled and said, "You are both welcome anytime." He held our hands and gave us a blessing and prayed for our journey and our futures.

The tractor departed and slowly went back down towards the car park. Along the way, Alfie said nothing, he was preoccupied, just looking out to the valley below. We finally reached the car park and got the coach back to the hostel.

That evening we sent our photos of our time in the town to a friend back home. We asked him to edit them, because we did not want grandad to know what had happened to his paradise.

After a few months it was time to head home. Once we arrived back, we visited our grandad.

We walked into his living room, and he looked up and said, "Haha, welcome home explorers, how was your journey?"
Alfie replied, "It was good grandad."
He asked, "And the town, did you go there?"
I said, "We did, and I have some photos for you; here look."
As he looked through our edited photos, he said, "I told you it was paradise didn't I. And look at how busy it is."
Alfie said, "I know, it was an amazing place and the people that we met were great."
He looked through the photos, then he stopped and held one photo towards his heart. He rested it there for a while, and then gazed at it, then quietly said, "Agnes, Agnes. She's still alive."
He looked at us and said, "Thank you, thank you so much, these photos are priceless."

Alfie got up and put his coat on, I asked, "Where are you going Alfie?"

He stopped; and then with a serious look on his face, he replied, "I think Ive got to go and find someone who is looking for me."

Jeremiah 29:13
You shall seek me. And you will find me, when you have sought me with your whole heart

Levende

Cry For Help

Running, racing, faster and faster, being chased, scrambling for my life.

'I am in danger.'

Screaming and continuously looking behind me because they are catching up with me.

Everyone in the street stops and stares, and no one tries to help me.

Can they not see what is happening to me, or do they not care?

My senses are alerted to the impending crisis that I find myself in.

This is a conspiracy to capture me.

I know it is.

I can see exactly what is happening here, I am no fool, and they are all part of it. This is a setup, and they're all in on it.

There is no time to take a breath, think, or speak; just run!

I am shaking with adrenaline.

"Where do I go, where, where?"

I see a car park ahead; I know I can take cover there.

I hurriedly start to race towards the entrance; I throw away my phone because they're tracking me.
If I can get to the top, I will be able to see everything and then I will have control of the situation.
I stop and try to rest, but I am nervous.
I know what they are trying to do to me; it is obvious.
Government agents, the doctors with their poison that they try to give me, and their scanning devices.
They can see all of us from behind mirrors and they listen to every word we say.
They're watching, always watching, but no one seems to believe me or wants to understand this.

Oh no!

They have found me.
A woman, and her young daughter disguised, pretending to be on a shopping trip with their bags.
I'm too clever for this;
do they honestly think I'm that stupid. They think I'm a fool.
Where to go; 'Think, Think', I could run to the stairs,

No!

They will be hiding in the stairwell.
 'The lift!'

No!

There are cameras all around; there is no easy escape.

There is a building on the opposite side of the car park.

I have to jump to safety, but I know I can make it away.

I creep between the parked cars and slowly towards the wall and rest to catch my breath.
Slowly standing up, I take one quick look around for danger, then;

1..2..3..Run………………uhh!

The following day, the News reported;

Yesterday a young man tragically lost his life when he appeared to fall from the 4th floor of a car park. The eyewitnesses described the man as agitated and screaming. He also said that he was being chased. However, there was no evidence that anyone was chasing him. Yet another sad end to a young life.

1 Peter 5-8:9
Be sober and vigilant. For your adversary, the devil, is like a roaring lion, travelling around and seeking those whom he might devour. Resist him by being strong in faith, being aware that the same passions afflict those who are your brothers in the world

Levende

Two Stones

In a hot barren desert, two stones baking in the sun formed part of a cliff edge, where they had been untouched for billions of years.

Over time, the landscape changed, but the two stones remained overlooking the vast area under the arid sun. Animals migrated, plants grew, shrivelled away and died, and eventually, people arrived over the course of many generations.

They built a small village on the vast land below the hills, and very slowly, stones started to fall away from the cliff edge, revealing new stone behind.

One day, the two stones fell from the cliff, tumbling down to the dusty ground below, lying there untouched. There they would have stayed, but for one day when some men carrying tools climbed the hill and started collecting rubble, stone and rock. The two stones were put into separate carts and brought down to the village below.

There, they were emptied into two large piles, and men sorted them according to size and quality. Every time the builders picked up the two stones, they were cast to the side again until, eventually one of the stones, the larger and smoother of the two, was placed on top of the building that the men had erected.

Once the work was completed, the people gathered in celebration to open this magnificent temple to God; however, the smaller of the two stones remained lying on top of a heap of discarded rubble that the builders could not find any use for.

A wealthy man built a house and used the smaller of the two stones as a step entering into an upper room, which he used to entertain guests.

Years went by, and the years turned into decades and the decades into centuries. The village grew into a town and eventually into a city. People went to the temple and lived their lives according to their teachings.

One by one, the people changed their religious beliefs, and fighting broke out. After many years of battling, the building became a Church.

The larger of the two stones remained on top of the building, shining like gold in the sun, whilst the other smaller stone now lay on the ground not far from the building, continuously being worn down and trampled on.

Not too many years later, another deadly battle broke out with men who came from the East, and after much loss of life the cross that adorned the top of the Church was pulled down, and another icon was placed on top.

For many years, people came to the building, and the larger stone sat proudly on top whilst the smaller stone was once again broken and cast out to the waste pile, disappearing under the sand and dirt.

Hundreds of years passed by, whilst regional wars claimed millions of innocent lives. Until finally a great war ripped through the entire world, tearing families apart, with brother fighting brother and father fighting son, leaving the land deserted. The once bustling city was now a crumbling ruin, fading from memory and being reclaimed by the desert sand.

However, one day the sun came up and lit the sky with a thousand colours. But as soon as it came up, thunder started to roar, and lightning began to strike, illuminating the sky. With this, all of the ground shook with an Almighty tremor and then; within a split second, like a conductor instructing his orchestra, the world fell

silent.

The ground trembled as the sound of footsteps came from behind where the building once stood tall. The larger stone was caught in the radiant light of the man who was standing before him.

The man walked past the crumbling building and then stopped. Looking around with his piercing brown eyes, he slowly crouched down and picked up a handful of dust and the smaller of the two stones.

The larger stone that once felt so important now looked on, watching the man with the broken smaller stone in his hand. The man continued to walk on, gathering up all that belonged to him.

1 Thessalonians 4:16-17

For the Lord himself, with a command and with the voice of an Archangel and with a trumpet of God, shall descend from heaven. And the dead, who are in Christ, shall rise up first. Next, we who are alive, who are remaining, shall be taken up quickly together with them into the clouds to meet Christ in the air. And in this way, we shall be with the Lord always.

One hour

8:45 am Driving into the lifeless corporate-built silicone-like city in a white corporate company EV, identical to every other car on the road and listening to the same uninspiring radio station as everyone else, playing the same "AI" tracks.

It is a monotonous work life that pays a ridiculous salary for doing little more than turning up, drinking coffee and playing golf on the office lawn.

While driving, I was thinking about our next vacation while trying to book a restaurant for tonight. Despite living in our house for 18 months, we still cannot figure out how to work the oven, and I forgot to get someone to clean the barbecue.

8:52 am My wife calls to say we need a new domestic cleaner. Maria quit this morning because she refused to clear my vomit out of the tub.

It was a heavy night!

I tell her, "Don't worry about it, just get another cleaner, and who does Maria think she is? She wasn't that good anyway. She always complained about her life, saying she had no money and her kids had nothing. The reason her kids have nothing is because she doesn't want to work two jobs, and her husband is 'depressed' because he doesn't work at all. He doesn't have a job because he's lazy." By this point, I am starting to raise my voice and lose my temper. "Why did you call me about this? You know my job is stressful. I've gotta go babe. I'll call you later, and please, please call a restaurant for tonight, ohh! and invite your friend Julia."

8:59 am I arrive at the office. I get out of the car and see Todd, who is my work and golfing buddy. "Hay Todd, we need to arrange a guy's weekend."

I swagger into the office building, which is now half empty because the other companies have either gone bust or are "relocating" to smaller premises. Maybe there will be a bit more room for us!

9:05 am I walk into our suite, grab a coffee, and slide into my office. I polish my scalp in the mirror and then sit back and swing my chair to look out the window.

Julia walks by, and I grab her attention. I beckon her into my office, and she sits in the opposite chair.

"Morning princess, did you enjoy last night? Honestly, at one point, I thought my wife would catch us. You're a bad influence on me."

"Chris, you're a bad influence on yourself. You don't know when to stop, and you definitely don't need my help, but if you want to get caught by your wife, that's fine with me."

She smiles and walks back out of the office to her desk.

9:17 am I see our manager walking down the hallway with seriousness written all over his face. I think to myself, 'Time to look busy.' I look at my screen and open my work, but then there is a knock on the door, and before I can look up, he is sitting in front of me.

"Morning Chris."

"Morning Paul," I replied. By the look on his face, I thought, 'Either his cat has died, he's got piles again, or his wife has finally left him.'

"Chris, I have been speaking to head office, and we need to make some changes."

'I thought, yeah about time Paul, get rid of the dead wood, and then maybe give me a pay rise, I need to pay for this vacation.'

He said, "The company as a whole is struggling, and we are going to downsize this branch. The unfortunate truth is we are going to have to let you go. This was a difficult decision, but I know you're financially secure. Some of the guys here are borrowing money to get to the end of the month as their pay cheque isn't enough. I'm sorry Chris; I hope you understand."

9:24 am He gets up, turns and walks away.

I sit there stunned, bewildered, and sick. I don't have any money saved, and I can barely afford the house. The car isn't mine, and the holidays are on the credit card. I'm finished!

My whole demeanour changes in that instant. I feel like I'm having an out-of-body experience, and my shoulders slump as if someone has just landed a 150-lb weight on me. They can't let me go, they can't do this to me. They're making me look like a fool.

I think for a while and collect my thoughts and composure.

Todd knocks on my door and walks in. I look at him and say, "Todd, not now, I've got too much on my mind."

"But Chris, have you heard what's happened?"

"Yeah, I have, but please, not now. This really isn't a good time."

Then Todd asked, "Chris, are you ok?"

"Yeah I'm fine. It's sad to hear some guys will be leaving us, but that's life I suppose. I'll catch up with you later."

Todd leaves the room and I gaze out of the window and think;
'What will I will do?
 What can I do?'
I don't think I have any options left.
It's checkmate and I have lost the game.'

9:37 a.m I stand up and take the car keys out of my pocket. I place them on the desk, write a note to my wife and then calmly walk out of my office and shut the door behind me.

9:39 am I go over to Julia, kiss her on the lips, and walk out to the main hall.

In a purposeful robotic style and without thinking, I leave the building and walk across the lawn with the sun beating down on my back; I walk through the trees and crawl under a wire fence. I walk onto the gravel track, sit down, cross my legs and close my eyes.

9:45 am I hear the train.

Proverbs 19:2
Where there is no knowledge of the soul, there is no good. And whoever hurries with his feet will stumble

If only Chris had paused for just one moment and spoken to Todd. If only he had shared his fear, it could have ended so differently, and it could have gone something like this:

My whole demeanour changes in that instant. I feel like I'm having an out-of-body experience, and my shoulders slump as if someone has just landed a 150-lb weight on me. They can't let me go, they can't do this to me. They're making me look like a fool.

I think for a while and collect my thoughts and composure.

Then in an act that I wouldn't normally do; I pause for a moment and pray! "If you're there God, I need you, more than ever before, I have been a fool and I've messed up." I look out the window, trying to figure out what to do.

Todd knocks on my door and walks in. "Hey Chris, have you heard what's happening?"
I look at him and he pauses then says,
"I'm sorry Chris, I didn't think he would let you go."
I replied, "Todd, I'm screwed. I have nothing; I'm broke, I don't know what to do, I literally have nothing to my name."

Todd replies, "I'm also leaving, I was leaving anyway. Paul wants me to stay, but I have had another offer. I know Paul didn't want to lose you, go and speak to him. If I am leaving then my position is vacant. Go and see him now!"

9:37 a.m I stand up and calmly walk out of my office and shut the door behind me.

9:39 am I go over to Julia and apologise for messing her around and say "I have to put everything right with my wife." I turn and walk out to the main hall.

In a less than a confident style and without thinking! I walk up the stairs to Paul's office. I knock on his door, and he asks me to enter. I explain my situation and I ask if Todd's position is available.

Paul offers me a chair, so I sit down and look towards the floor, I cross my legs and close my eyes.

9:45 am I hear Paul say, "I would be delighted if you would stay with us."

Meanwhile outside the window, we hear the train go by.

Relief rushes through my body, and I think, 'It's strange how quickly an hour can change everything.

Proverbs 3:5-6

Trust in the Lord with all your heart. Never rely on what you think you know. Remember the Lord in everything you do, and he will show you the right way.

Always Remember to Talk

Levende

Angel whisper peace to me

Standing by the water's edge, looking out towards the sea. Watching the thunderous turquoise and black waves roll in, crashing into the rocks below. I marvel and can only imagine the enormity of the waves and how unimaginable God must be; to be able to tame the sea and all its might.

Unaware of any impending danger, and as I look out, I am overcome. Within an instant, I am turning and rolling in fear. I have lost all of my senses; I don't know which way is up or which way is down, the swell of the sea has engulfed me, and I am grasping for my life. I am in pure shocked and so confused that I do not even feel the cold of the sea, but the taste of salt compounds my fear.

I pray that someone will rescue me.

Trying in vain to gasp for air, but only filling my lungs with the cold salty water.

I am slowly pulled down, away far below the surface, until the light begins to disappear, vanishing from my sight.
I stop kicking and punching out with fright, trying to save my own life. The waves that without mercy, were crashing down on top of me now look so calm.

The swirling sea falls still, and I give up my fight. I am losing my life, and I can feel myself starting to let go.

'Oh Angel, Whisper peace to me.'
The sea grows darker until I can see no more.

'Stillness,.. darkness,….lifeless,…..gone.'

Then,….…..a light shining brightly above me releases me from this darkness. A hand reaches down and pulls me to safety, out of the sea and into the arms of my saviour.

He walks me across the water to the shore.
To a new land, to a new life.

I am home.

Jonah 2:6-8

The waters surrounded me, even to the soul. The abyss has walled me in. The ocean has covered my head. I descended to the base of the mountains. The bars of the earth have enclosed me forever. And you will raise up my life from corruption, Lord, my God. When my soul was in anguish within me, I called to mind the Lord, so that my prayer might come to you, to your holy temple

To fall in love

I so vividly remember the first time I set my eyes on her, not knowing what to do or think. I was totally awestruck and so naively and easily drawn in. And then; very gently and so very softly, she seductively kissed me; instantly taking my breath away.

I couldn't believe it was possible to have such an intense feeling, to feel completely absorbed and yet detached from any reality. The following day all I could do was to think about her; the way she looked and the sweet smell of her, and the way she could so quickly and easily draw me in.

I thought to myself, 'Tonight, I will kiss her one last time, and then I will just keep her as a memory.'

So again, that evening she kissed me, and I could feel her run through every inch of my body, giving me an unquenchable thirst. I was utterly and completely blown away by her.

I was, without wanting to be, desperately and shamefully in love. Every waking hour all I could do was think about was her; the way she could take me higher and higher, before dropping me like a stone. I couldn't cope without her not being near me, the way she made me feel so complete, making me feel so alive.

The following day I decided that I wanted to introduce her to my girlfriend.

I didn't know how she would react, but Sofia said she wanted to meet her.

So late one evening, I thought the time was right. I arrived at Sofia's house and after waiting for several minutes, the wrought iron gates finally swung open allowing me to drive up the long drive to the large house. Sofia met me by the door and asked me to come in and say hello to her parents.

She kissed her mum and dad goodbye; her dad told her that he loved her and to be careful. He looked at me with no expression, and then turned back and squeezed her hand. She kissed him on the forehead, and then we left her home.

We arrived at my apartment, and I took Sofia straight into my bedroom. After a while I brought my new lover into the room and with no hesitation, she very gently kissed Sofia. As we lay on my bed, I could see the excitement run through Sofia's eyes.

"What is her name?" Sofia asked,

"Heroin" I replied.

It was like falling in love for the first time every time, yet hating your lover. Like a bullet to the brain, my head exploding with relief, giving total fulfilment before my reality returns.

Sofia lays naked beside me, her face transfixed with the satin bed sheets barely covering her perfect silk body, making love to our new best friend in her own sensual ethereal way.

Seconds, minutes, and hours pass by. In total fulfilment, I look across the bed towards Sofia, with whom I have shared my bed, my body and my drug.

Sofia now lays stone-cold dead beside me, her eyes vacant,
but she is still staring at me.

"Oh God;

What have I done?"

Wisdom 1:12-13
Do not court death by the error of your life, nor procure your destruction by the works of your hands,   because God did not make death, nor does he rejoice in the loss of the living

Levende

Forgiveness

In a childlike innocent way I lay deathly still, with battle-drenched bloody mud wrapping itself around me like a blanket, though offering no comfort at all.

The smell of the smoked filled air terrifies me, and with the stench of death it creates a veil, and fear compounds my senses with an Orchestra of Death clashing and ringing in my ears.

I slowly stand, bewildered and shaking; uncontrollably shaking. I am so frightened.

My fingers tremble and I am tormented by every thought that runs through my broken mind, as I gently caress the trigger. I see before me the war-torn bloody battlefield, stripped of all humanity as we walk through an abandoned playground, and ironically the swing still sways and the church bell tolls.

I am,….. I am so scared.

The night sky, lit by the fireworks of war as we run in total fear towards our enemy, shells falling all around us, the vibration almost ripping through my chest and tearing up my body.

Lights race towards us with a deafening 'Crackle' and friends fall motionless to the ground. Another light brighter than the others stares straight into my face.

My whole world is now in slow motion, but the light is yet not past me.

I feel so hot!

I look at my stomach, and there, I see blood burning my skin. I collapse under the weight of my humbled body to my knees, yet the light is still before me.

I want to go home; I don't belong here.

Tears are now washing my broken face and blurring my vision. "Mom, I'm so sorry, I'm so sorry, Mom."

I look to my side; I see Joey calmly walking on by, with no gun in his hand and no fear in his eyes.

I don't understand. "What are you doing Joey? Joey, get down." He comes to my side, kneels down beside me, and helps me to my feet, and we walk on together.

Now, many of our friends are running past us, completely unaware of our presence, screaming, shouting and firing towards the enemy, and their armoured cars and tanks

We continue to walk. Bullets unable to harm us, shells no longer slam me into the ground.

Fear? I don't feel it!

Beyond the light that I see before us, I notice other men coming from the opposite direction, walking towards the same translucent light.

The man who filled me with lead is now walking with me in complete silence.

Before me, I see a hand outstretched towards us beckoning us to come closer.

Wisdom 4-7

But the just, if death seizes him beforehand, will be refreshed

Levende

Kings Cross

Exhausted, I slowly open my eyes and stretch out. Every single one of my muscles cries out 'Leave me alone'.

I rub my weary eyes and yawn. Then, I sit up and open my bottle of warm stale water. I sit there for a while, trying to gather my thoughts, and put my head into gear.

I then roll over and stumble to my feet like a drunken ballerina; whilst trying to find some balance before spinning around and falling into the wall.

All my friends laugh at me, saying "Go on Swanny, you can make it if you try!"

With that 'morning' blurred vision, I look around and think, 'Here we go again,'another hard day in the office'.

I achingly wander over to my spot whilst scratching like a dog. I sit back down and watch people go by whilst I relax on my faux cardboard sofa up against a wall of solid cold concrete.

I do not need a watch; I can tell what the time is by observing the same people passing by on their way to work, strangely in the same order most days. Laughing to myself, I think, 'Cows will go into the milking parlour in the same order every day; this is a human farm yard.' I know who will acknowledge me with a smile, who will look at me with disgust and who will ignore my existence. Some people will cleverly kick me, thinking that no one will notice or even care.

I never ask for money and I rarely receive it. I can't play an instrument, and I cannot sing. I have nothing to offer so I don't ask for help; I don't want to be a burden on anyone. I like to see the world in motion, to watch people and observe the same continuous habits that we all have. I like the uniqueness that individually we possess.

As I watch, looking over people from my throne. I often examine my conscience because I have plenty of time to kill, doing little or nothing else. I am the therapist and the nutcase rolled into one. Looking and trying to find answers to the deep, unanswered questions like an unemployed and uneducated Philosopher.

I believe, or at least I hope, that I am intelligent, honest, and sincere. I just unknowingly and very quickly lost the person that I once was, along with everyone else here sitting with me. All of us here justify our own lives because there is no one to challenge us.

However, there is a young Irish woman called Claire. She passes by on her way to work and brings me a cup of coffee and a croissant every morning without fail. She treats me with respect that I find hard to hold for myself. I am embarrassed when talking to her, but I look forward to seeing her every morning. She reminds me of a family I no longer have.

She will come over to me, bend down and say:
"Good morning; how are you today?"
I reply, "I am very well thank you."
"That's good to hear; I hope you have a nice day."
"Thank you Claire."
Then she will go on her way, and I feel thankful to have her as my only friend.

However, on one bitterly cold night, whilst buried in my sleeping bag, which I usually wouldn't zip up. I felt something heavy hit me in the head. Before I could work out what was happening, I felt another blast to my back, which made me lurch forward and then a kick into my stomach; I was being attacked.

I tried to curl up to protect myself, but the viciousness prevented me from doing so, and the voices started shouting at me, "You worthless piece of scum, vermin, time to die, kill him."

I just lay there, unable to get out of my sleeping bag, which was meant to protect me, thinking this is it; this is where I am going to die. The punching and kicking is relentless; but then it stops and I hear the sound of liquid pouring onto my sleeping bag and with it, laughter. The liquid starts to penetrate the bag and runs down my face. 'I am a grown man.'
I am numb!
Then as motionless as I can be, I start to cry in silence.

Then I pass out.

I try to open my eyes, but I can't, and I am hurting with indiscriminate pain. My eyelids feel heavy, and I feel so weak. I try to cough, but even that hurts. I hear a voice saying, 'Shhhhhh!' Then, as hard as I try, the only word I can whisper is "Where?" and the voice says, "Hospital."

I am safe!

She wets my lips and holds my hand as I drift back to sleep.

A few days later, and as I woke up, I could just about open one of my eyes to see. A nurse came to see me and I thanked her for staying with me and comforting me whilst I slept.

With a warm smile, she said, "That was not me, that was your daughter."
"But I don't have a daughter."
She replied, "Well, she was here earlier, and I believe she will be back again soon."
I lay there confused. I thought that the nurse must have been thinking of another patient. A while later, as I was resting, I heard a chair move in close beside me; I looked up and sat beside me was this young woman who would buy me coffee every morning.

She held my hand.

I asked, "Why are you here?"
She replied, "I knew someone was attacked at the station that evening, and when you were not where you would normally be, I became concerned. The following morning I knew it had to be

you, so I came searching for you; I was worried! My children have made you some get-well cards."

I had no words that could express my gratitude to her.

She said, "You are not going back there to live. I have found somewhere for you to call home. I don't want to lose you."

Matthew 25:35-36

For I was hungry, and you gave me to eat; I was thirsty, and you gave me to drink; I was a stranger, and you took me in, naked, and you covered me; sick, and you visited me; I was in prison, and you came to me.

Levende

Gunnild

Once upon a time, there was a land that was so perfect.

Everyone was called a friend and a man was a friend to everyone. The world was as it was meant to be, and they all lived for each other.

At this time, there was also a husband and wife who lived on a farm just outside a village, on a hill overlooking their friends who lived in the houses below.

Day and night the husband would tirelessly work coming up with new ideas and inventions. He would sometimes call his friends to show them his newest and, 'always' his greatest idea that would transform their lives.

One night, whilst the village slept, he could not rest. Tossing and turning until a lightbulb moment raced into his head. He quickly jumped out of his bed with pure excitement, and in a frenzy, he rushed to his old wooden workshop.

He pulled open the large oak doors, lit the lantern and started to cut, bend, weld and screw until he stood back in amazement and thought to himself, 'This is, without question, the most incredible, the best, the most fantastic and useful idea yet.'

He was so proud, and he could not sleep for the rest of the night, just waiting for the sun to come up and the cockerel to crow, so he could rush down to the village below, call his friends, and show them how he was going to change their lives forever.

His friends were partly puzzled but amazed by this clever invention, but not sure of its purpose, though they all agreed hunting would be so much easier.

However, an elderly man was visiting the village on this day. He was not as excited as the others and wasn't sure that the object would be of any great benefit. The other people just said he was old and crazy, lost in his mind.

The following day, the old man visited the man on his farm and his new invention. He warned him of the power that this tool could bring but also that no good could come from it. The man just smiled and told him not to worry too much.

Later that evening, as the man slept peacefully in bed, a noise startled him. With no reason to worry, he fell back to sleep.

In the morning, he woke to find the door to his workshop wide open; he hurriedly got dressed and went outside. As he entered the workshop, it was obvious that his best idea was nowhere to be seen. Angered by this, he went down into the village and confronted everyone, shouting and screaming as it had become apparent that someone had taken something that did not belong to them. This had never happened before; somebody was dishonest.

The old man just watched as people also started to show their anger, something that had never been seen before. He felt sorrow for what he could see. This object had brought nothing good to the village.

A few days later, while the man was working in his workshop, his neighbour walked in holding the greatest invention in his hand. The man looked up to greet him and saw his invention, thinking his neighbour had found it; he began to smile.

Without warning, his neighbour raised the invention, pulled the trigger, and released the hatred from the barrel.

A bullet raced towards the man and ripped through his skin before it tore straight through his body.

The man slowly fell back, as if caught in someone's arms, and came to rest on the ground.

He lay there dying, crumpled on the sawdust floor, and his neighbour watched on as he died.

When the dead man's wife heard the news, she was overcome with grief; not only had her husband died, but his friend had killed him. She fell to her knees, and in anger, which she had never felt before, she shouted out to God, "Who are you? What are you? Where are you? Why have you done this to me?"

The old man came to her side and knelt beside her, "God did not invent the weapon, he did not place it into your neighbour's hand, and he did not pull the trigger. It was free will that killed him."

The following day, the woman woke from her broken sleep with tears soaking her pillow. She rose from her bed and looked out of her window; everything was the same as the day before as if the world was unaware of her loss or did not care.

The woman wanted to thank the old man for calming her down and helping her feel some peace. She went down to the village, and try as she might, he was nowhere to be seen. She asked the villagers, but no one had ever heard of or seen a man of his description; they told her, "When you were kneeling down crying, there was no one by your side."
She turned away and returned to her home.

James 4-1
Where do wars and contentions among you come from? Is it not from this: from your own desires, which battle within your members

We're Only Human

Walking home after a night out with some friends.

My mind was wandering, thinking about my job, my wife, and my children, who are now growing up so quickly. Life has rushed by, getting faster and faster, and I feel I have lost control.

As I walked along, I heard a scream from behind, followed by a loud crash and then, for a split second, complete silence.

Then, the silence was broken by the sound of pure mayhem.

I turned around to see what had happened. To my horror, a young child was lying motionless in the middle of the road with a car's headlights illuminating the scene. I ran over to the child, and as I bent down, I saw blood trickling from his ears. I held his hand, and as I looked at him, I could see nothing could be done; at that moment, I felt inadequate and helpless. I stayed with him, letting him see a calm in my face, disguising my despair whilst everyone else was screaming and shouting. I prayed with him, knowing there was nothing else that I could do.

The emergency services arrived and after the police questioned me, I watched the paramedics take his body away, after which I was then allowed to go home.

I wandered the streets for hours in disbelief, trying to make sense of something that made no sense at all. As I returned home, as quietly as I could, I opened the front door, took my shoes off, and my wife came down the hall and shouted at me. She asked why I hadn't replied to any of her calls and wanted to know who I had been with, as all my friends had returned home three hours before.

Not wanting to get into a conversation, I simply said that I went for a walk.

I stumbled into the shower, slid down into the corner, put my hands over my face and cried. I sobbed, broke my heart and then cried some more. Once my wife fell asleep, I got dried and slid into bed. I lay there motionless for 5 hours, just staring at nothing, with the child's face etched into my mind.

Over the next couple of weeks, my life was on stop! I was in a zombie-like mode. I couldn't think, I didn't want to think! What was there to think about?

When I decided to return to work, I was called into the office. I had a meeting and a conversation without understanding what was being said to me. I did not reply to the questions being asked of me and did not care about anything anyway. I was flatlining with a heartbeat.

On Sunday, as on every other Sunday, we went to church as a family. I sat there listening intently, trying to understand what was being said, but it may have been in another language. I thought, 'I don't believe it anymore; I don't believe it.' Like a candle extinguished, my faith collapses within one sentence like a deck of cards, and I don't care.

I get up quietly, go outside and light a cigarette. I sit there for a while wondering what has happened to me, 'This was not only my faith, but it was my life, and now it's gone. I don't feel anything, nothing.

It's gone!

I decided to walk down a few streets, eventually entering a neighbourhood I didn't know. I went into a bar and ordered a beer. I sat there, looking into the faded mirror behind the optics, which were there for no other purpose than to forget while shuffling the cigarette pack between my fingers.

I noticed a guy sitting at the other end of the bar drinking water, and after a while, we got talking. Within an hour, it is as if we have been friends our whole lives, talking about nothing but everything with little value. Eventually, he said he had to go; as he walked out, he said it was good talking.

I ask him his name;

He replies, "Mo."

"Goodnight Mo."

The following evening after work, I returned to the bar as I wanted to avoid the barrage of questions and interrogation at home. Opening the door, I spotted Mo, and his face lit up. We sat in the bar talking for hours, and within a month, we became close friends. He knows about my life and how I once had a Christian faith, and I know about his life and how he was also once a man of faith.

One evening, he invited me to his apartment for a meal, and to watch the football. I arrived, and as his wife prepared the food, she took me by the hand and said, "Thank you for coming. Mo has been so lost recently, and I have been desperately concerned about him. I am so grateful that he has found a good friend." She walked out and left us to watch the game.

As I was sitting there, my eyes were drawn to a photo of a boy on the wall.
I looked at it and away again; however, I was drawn back to it again and again, and so I asked,

"Mo, tell me, who is the boy in this picture?"
"That was my son 'Adam', but he is now dead."
I replied, "I'm so sorry."

His eyes glazed up as he looked at the picture and said that he was killed by a car last January.

I looked at the photo and then looked at Mo and said, "Mo, I was with him when he died; I prayed with him and stayed with him till the end. I am so sorry."

Mo looked at me, "It was you! I asked who was with him when he died, but the police wouldn't tell me."

I'm dumbstruck!

Proverbs 16-9

The heart of man disposes his way. But it is for Lord to direct his steps

Levende

The Text

Anyway, my parents are kinda strict; they don't understand much apart from ordering me around. I personally think they missed their anti-natal classes because they're so out of their depth. I sometimes sit down to start gaming, and they're on my back already; I seriously don't know what to do with them. My friends don't get this sort of abuse, and their parents get me!

I mean, I must have been adopted; there can be no other explanation; they're both so weird.

I caught my dad feeling my mom's ass, calling it a 'right peach.' What's wrong with the man? he totally grossed me out, and then he tried to hug me! I had to scrub my face afterwards; that was just so totally and completely wrong on every level.

I had to confront him about his behaviour because I just could not tolerate it any longer.

Big mistake, I mean seriously a huge mistake, one that I would soon regret!

After voicing my strong disapproval, they both told me it was their home, they brought me into the world through a "loving" relationship, and I was still their child.

My jaw dropped. I was totally speechless, and I thought, 'Are you both completely insane?' I raised my hand, and pointed my finger at them both as Dad would do to me, and then said, "Enough is enough; this has to stop, and it stops now. Understand!"

Anyway!

Five minutes later, I found myself packing my bag as I was off to stay with my dad's uncle. I didn't even know he had an uncle!

My world was falling apart.

Once I finished packing, I said goodbye to Mom, and she tried to kiss me, only to humiliate me I guess. I got in the car and put my ear pods straight in so I could avoid any conversation with Dad. He tried to speak, but he soon got the idea.

After some hours of driving to nowhere, we came to a monastery. I didn't know why we were there, so I decided not to ask.

Dad got out of the car, went up to the door and rang the bell. An older man came to the door and hugged Dad.

Reality was dawning on me, and it wasn't a reality I wanted to consider.

My dad called me from the car; and he said, "This is Uncle Mike."

I thought you have got to be kidding—a monk! You have never told me about this uncle, and then it dawned on me—this religious nut must be as crazy as you are.

Dad looked at me as if he wanted me to say something. What do you expect me to say? So I just gave the smallest smile that I thought I could get away with.

Total humiliation!

Before my brain could catch up, Dad said goodbye, hugged me and got back in the car. He drove off down the long driveway, and I just watched in disbelief; then, this man that I didn't know asked me to follow him inside. Before we went in, he asked for my phone, "I don't have one!" was my clever reply.
He just smiled, "Phone, please."
I gave him my phone.
"How's your mom? She's a total peach."

I couldn't believe it!

We went in, and he showed me to my room, which it would appear they forgot to furnish, and 'the TV must have been in a cupboard,' but I didn't want to ask.

I met all of these other men who appeared to be excited to see me; I am feeling totally freaked out!

After finding my way around and having a meal, I went to bed early to watch TV.

'No TV!

The following day, I was told I would be working with several monks—first, the carpenter.

This tall thin man, Father John, took me into a workshop where he was repairing a stained glass window. He showed me where the rot had been destroying the wood, and he asked me to remove the rot very carefully until I found the wood again.

So that is precisely what I did; we were both working in silence, with no radio, no talking, nothing! Then he asked me how I was getting on,
"Okay, I guess," was the only reply I could think of.
He came over to have a look and said, "Well done; you know it is important to remove all of the rot; otherwise, if any is left, it will not be a complete repair. Wood and people are similar in ways. If someone does you wrong, it is important to find forgiveness as soon as possible; like us here now, we must chisel out all the rotten wood as soon as we find it. If we don't, the timber will rot and be lost."

"I suppose so," I replied. Though "Weirdo" was what I was thinking.

After we finished removing the rot and sealing the wood, he told me to go for lunch.

On the way to the dining room, I saw Uncle Mike; he asked, "How are you settling in?" "Okay, I guess," was again the only reply I could think of.

I reached the dining room; I was so thirsty and desperate for a drink that I picked up a cup of water and started to drink it. As soon as it passed my lips, I spat it out, "Shit, it's boiling," was the first thing that I said.

Laughter came from behind me, 'Oh crap' was my first thought, "You didn't want to do that did you." this man replied, whilst laughing, with a massive smile on his face.
"No, I didn't, and I'm sorry for,"
"Oh, don't worry about that; are you okay?"
"Yeah, I think so," I replied.
"I am Father Leo; that cup was for my herbal tea; now come and help prepare the table for lunch."

As we put everything in its place, Father Leo placed some large jugs of cold water on the table and poured a drink for us both.
"Tell me, why are you here,"
"I don't know, my dad thought I needed some time out maybe, though I think by the way he was grabbing my mom, he just wanted me gone for a couple of days for his own convenience."
"Oh, they must love each other then, That's good" was his reply.
I just looked at him and thought, 'That's sick.'

"Your mom and dad's relationship is like this jug of water,"
'You're just weird' was my only thought, and I rolled my eyes. Then he went on,

"Love and hate are like this.
Love.
Turn on the tap and pour some water, pure and cold; it quenches your thirst.
Hate.
Turn on the tap, fill the kettle, and soon the water will boil.

Now unable to drink it, for it will scorch your mouth, as you now know.

Love is instant and pure.

Hatred takes time to boil and has no form of purity left within it.

It is far easier to drink straight from the cup."

He was right, and I actually listened to him.

That evening, when clearing the dinner table, I spotted my phone in a drawer. I quickly threw it into my pocket and told everyone that I was tired and was off to bed.

Once I got to my room, I pulled out my phone to text Tommy and let him know what was happening to me:

Text

'ha Tommy I dont kn0 wot R trying 2 do 2 me man, bt theres some straNg schet goin on & dEz fellas starting 2 frEk me out.

Dont txt cuz dey have kidnapped my fone.'

Translated

'Hey, Tommy, I don't know what they are trying to do to me man! but there's some strange shit going on, and these guys are starting to freak me out. Don't text back because they have kidnapped my phone.'

The following day, after breakfast, I quickly returned my phone to where I found it. Then Uncle Mike asked me to go with Father Francis to help him finish his work. Father Francis was 28 years old and had a recognisable face. He told me that he used to be a DJ and lived life to an extreme level and loved raves.

Seriously! I didn't know if I could believe him or not. However, he knew the answers to everything when I questioned him, and he was the coolest guy I had ever met.

We went for a walk, and he told me to walk barefoot with him. We sat on a bench and just totally chilled out for a while. He told me to take in all the sounds of nature, to listen to the volume of the silence, to feel everything around me and to relax. He said that the sound of nature is the greatest rave of our lives.

After a while, he led me into a studio in the gardens. The place was covered in art. This guy is not only a DJ but also an awesome artist.

He said that we had to frame a painting that he had recently sold and was then sending it abroad. We took the canvas and laid it out, ready to be framed.

Whilst he was examining the painting, he said, "You know, every one of us is like a flick of a paintbrush, making up a whole painting, and it is not until the masterpiece is complete that you can see the full picture. The painting could be of Christ, and as for you, you could be the twinkle in his eye. So we must never despair with who we are or what we have; trust in God, and all will be."

I looked at him and then realised Uncle Mike and my dad were not as crazy as I thought; maybe it was me going mad.

Father Francis then said, "It is so important just to stop for a short while and clear our minds, a little like emptying the trash on a PC and then carrying on with our day, with our minds cleared. Listen, do not let yourself crash." He then told me that it was time for us to go.

I hurried back to the kitchen and grabbed my phone; I went outside and texted Tommy.

Text

'Ha Tommy did U kn0 dat wen U git ^ ear1E n d morn d graS iz wet evN tho it hasn't Bin raining, dey caL it dew & d birds will cum & sit dwn bside U & jst watch U.'
Savage mang
God Bless dud

Translated
'Hey Tommy, Did you know that when you get up early in the morning the grass is wet, even though it hasn't been raining, they call it dew and the birds will come and sit down beside you and watch you, Savage man!
God bless dude.

Uncle Mike found me and said my dad would be here within an hour and I should collect my belongings.
"No," was the only reply I could think of.

As I collected my things, I turned to Uncle Mike and said, "The one thing I still find weird is that you called Mom 'A Peach'."

He laughed and said, "Everyone calls her Peach; she hates her middle name, so it's a family joke."

"No!" I said with surprise and laughter, "I didn't know that was her middle name!" and we both laughed. I said goodbye to everyone; I couldn't believe I was leaving.

Father Francis took my phone and put a link on it, "Play this on your way home."

I got in the car, and my dad drove away. I opened the link that Father Francis gave me, and it was of him as the DJ at a rave that I had watched so many times before.

I knew I recognised him!

I just smiled.

Proverbs 3:5-6
Have confidence in the Lord with all your heart, and do not depend upon your own prudence. In all your ways, consider him, and he himself will direct your steps.

Levende

Complete

The hurt,   the pain,   the dagger piercing, twisting through my torn and broken mortal body, and into my wretched undeserving soul. Weighing me down like never before.

Why do I hurt so badly?
No tears left to cry!
No emotion left to burn,
and no excitement for the things that we used to do.
I am   so   completely and utterly alone, shattered and destroyed.

Even sadness and sorrow have deserted me.
Turning their backs on me, and closing the door on their way out,
in total disgust.

I have Nothing!
I am Nothing.
Just a shell, void of a life that used to be.

Why; why am I so empty? And when will this torment end?

I am scared to live; but yet, I do not want to die.

Levende

I have no strength; I'm done!

Trying to function is no longer possible or even wanted, and I never realised that gravity could be so heavy.

Inside;   inside I have already died.

Why is my life a living hell?
Am I the only one ever to feel this way?
Why; when I have hit the bottom am I still falling?
And why do I feel like I am fighting the entire world all by myself?
Why?
I don't understand.

What is life trying to do to me? To destroy me? Well life, I have news for you: You're too late!

I feel completely abandoned by life, exiled and alone, I have been played like a fool!

All I want,
All I want is to feel normal.
To feel wanted.
To feel……….. love.   Something that's free but somehow evades me.
I want to feel worthy.
I'm so tired.
I am so tired of this world judging me.
I can't do this anymore!

All I want,…….I don't even know what I want.

I want something more than this.
To feel complete.

Then a voice whispers; "Come closer to me."
With tears filling my eyes, I scream out in my head,
"How?
I DON'T KNOW WHERE YOU ARE?"

Lord, help me……help me please!
I need you.
Be merciful with me.
Please.

Matthew 27-45:46

Now from the sixth hour, there was darkness over the entire earth, even until the ninth hour. And about the ninth hour, Jesus cried out with a loud voice, saying: "Eli, Eli, lamma sabacthani?" that is, "My God, My God, why have you forsaken me?

Levende

Herengracht

Aimlessly, I am yet again wandering through the colourful cobbled streets that I have come to know so well, trying to escape the city heat whilst watching people as they pass me by. They briefly walk into my life and straight back out again on a human conveyor belt.

Workers, tourists, families, friends and strangers on holiday tapping their cards or phones on the payment machines with no care or any idea about how much they are spending. Today's Motto 'Live for today because tomorrow never comes'.

As for myself, that was also once my reality, but my tomorrow did catch up with me and threw me out of the ring like a boxer who didn't see the final punch coming. As for now, now! I am like an expired credit card with no value to anyone. The funny thing is, I am now completely invisible, as if I have been erased, brushed out and forgotten. Life has just raced on without me, and I realise I am just another dispensable product of this consumer race called life.

As I make my way through the streets, I try to keep my distance from the cafes because people only see a homeless person, and I am judged without defence. Also, the smell on offer from the cafes is too expensive, and it triggers memories that I no longer need or want.

However, one day in May, as I was minding my own business, I stopped by a cafe because I had an aggravating stone in my boot. How it got in there, I don't know. I stopped, and sat on a small wall filled with spring flowers and removed my stinking boot. As I did, I noticed a woman looking at me. She was watching intently but not intrusively, just looking at what I was doing. I shook out my boot and put it back on. I sat there momentarily, smelling the coffee-fragranced air floating out of the cafe. The woman was just….looking, watching, reading me. After a moment, I got back up and carried on my way.

A few days later, drenched in an unexpected shower, I was going by the same cafe, and again, the same familiar fragrance filled the air. Ironically yet again, I felt another stone digging into my foot. Again, I stopped by the same wall; the rain stopped and I took my boot off and shook it out. As I looked up, I saw the same woman sitting in the same place; this time though she was smiling at me. I looked back at her, now slightly annoyed because I was frustrated about having to do up my frail laces once again, that were ready to snap.

She looked over to me and with a soft gentle voice said, "It must be annoying when you tie your boots so tight, yet a stone can still work its way in."

I looked at her and said, "That's exactly what I was thinking."

She got up and started to walk away, then turned to me and said, "Would you be kind enough to help me with my bag? I am only going down the road."

I agreed and took her bag and we started to walk in silence. Me hobbling and now trying to hide my pain and frustration until we reached a small door nestled between two narrow, but tall old buildings. Above the door was a small wooden plaque which read, *'é tudo para ele'*. There was no door handle, key, or number on the door. I remember thinking that I had never noticed it before, but then again, why would I?
I asked her, "How do you get in?"

She looked at me with pity, as if I were a "little" stupid and said, "It is simple; you knock."

'Oh yeah', I thought, 'That makes sense you idiot!'

I gave the bag to her and turned to walk away.

She called out, "Where are you going?"

I looked back, hesitated and replied, "I don't know?"

She looked at me and said, "Come in, and I will find a lace for your boot."

I agreed as I had nowhere to go.

She knocked on the door, and an elderly man answered. We walked into a narrow corridor less than a metre wide but carried on for probably 60 metres. There were no windows, lights, or candles flickering, but it wasn't dark, which confused me. I knew the light had to be coming from somewhere, but where? I had no idea. I followed her to a room on the right-hand side and went in. There was an old desk with a vase filled with flowers; she opened the desk drawer, and inside was a single shoelace; she took it and handed it to me.

Bewildered, I asked her why the desk was empty except for one shoelace, and she replied, "Did you want something else?"
"No" I replied.
We sat down while I changed the lace, and she asked me, "Why did you come in?"
"Because you asked me."
She sat there for a while in deep thought and finally said, "Come with me."

We got up, and I followed her as she sped down the corridor—me, limping, skipping, jumping, just trying to keep up. Finally we reached a larger double door; she opened it and walked in. I stood at the entrance in amazement. The room was colossal, with a vaulted ceiling, and a blue and gold dome that appeared to continuously rise up and fade into a vail of mist within the roof above. There were many people all appearing to have a purpose.

"What is this place? I know this area of the city so well, and this just shouldn't fit in. It makes no sense to me at all." There's a tiny door on the street, and now this. "What is going on, and who are you?"

"I help those who ask to be helped, and this building belongs to my Son; I help him with his business".

"What sort of business does your son run?"
She said, "Come and help me here. Please take this box to the canal and leave it on the side. Someone else will come to collect it later. Once you have finished, hurry back, and don't let anyone see you."

"Why?" I replied.
She just looked at me and reminded me of my mother.

I picked up the box and did as she asked, which I did for the next six months, helping the homeless and anyone in need.

Finally, one day she came and sat beside me on a step with her hands on her knees. She smiled and said, "I believe it is time for you to go back home to your family."

I sighed.
"I can't" I replied.

She smiled, then looked into my eyes and said,
"You must, and you know you should. You could quite easily stay here, but you are stopping yourself from what you truly desire; your family, and they need you.
I will be with you. Remember that I love you like my own child. You are mine.
You are perfect, but you just became lost. Well, I found you, so you can no longer be lost."

Though I was sad, I knew she was right.

Then she said, "Always remember to knock on the door, even if you think no one will answer. The door will always be opened."

The following day, I got ready, said my goodbyes and walked back out of that tiny front door that once welcomed me, and back onto the cobbled street. As I walked away, I turned back for one last look, but all I could see were the two narrow tall buildings and a drinking fountain with fresh water where the tiny door had been. I smiled to myself and carried on. As I walked past the cafe, I saw a man frustratingly banging a stone out of his boot; as she sat on a chair outside the cafe. She looked up and with a mother's love, she smiled at me.

John 2:5
His mother said to the servants, "Do whatever he tells you."

Superhero

It's crazy; I'm barely 19 years old.

Here I am, waiting nervously, sitting on a concrete bench in a long narrow clinical lobby with my Dad and some friends. Waiting to be called into an inquest, and it feels as though time has stopped. My legs shake, and I twiddle with my fingers, trying to bite my fingernails that I have already destroyed.

I can't believe that we are here.

I wish I could go back to when I was a kid again. Life was so easy and uncomplicated. On Saturday mornings, we would go to the cinema and watch an action movie, somehow finding enough money between us to buy some popcorn and throw it at the girls sitting in front of us, trying to impress them and showing off our undeniably cool status.

The movie was always about some guy saving the world in some stupid but incredible way, repeated a thousand times in different stories; he was always invincible and almost ultra-human.

However, we were always drawn into each film believing in the unbelievable, wanting to be that guy who was out of reach, wishing our lives would emulate that of the hero or villain, and just wanting to make our lives something more than merely existing.

After a few years of watching films, playing online and slowly getting older, we were left with a void in our lives; we needed a Rush. We needed the thrill that would leave us feeling like we were living our lives, that of the make-believe Hero.

As the years went on, we eventually started daring each other to do stupid things that we thought were cool and also to make us laugh. Eventually, we began to steal cars, free climb in our city or any other city if we could get there, and basically do anything that would give us that feeling that we desperately craved. Occasionally, we would get stoned—'or maybe more than occasionally'.

Our parents would go crazy, blaming everyone else's son but their own, trying to turn us against each other but only strengthening our friendship; we were no longer kids, but they thought differently. We would upload our videos, and we had a growing online following. Everything was good, and life was becoming exciting.

On a Sunday morning, we decided to climb a suspension bridge around 30 miles away from home. It wasn't a big climb, around 80 feet from the road to the top of the tower. The four of us assessed the dangers and then started to ascend. We reached the top and stood on the wide plinth. There was a breeze; you could feel it, but nothing more than we were used to. As we stood there filming each other and the buildings in the distance, Matteo decided to do a backflip; it was his trademark, which he always did when possible. We got our cameras ready, and we were all excited. Matteo threw himself into the air, flipped over and landed, but he didn't realise he had landed on the edge of the plinth. As he stood there, he punched the air and took a step back, and that was it;

He was gone!

We looked at each other for a split second in disbelief and then scrambled to where he fell. We looked over the edge, expecting him to be just below, laughing. But there he was, 80 feet below, lying on the road.

We all went crazy, shouting at him to get up and screaming at each other. I called my Dad and told him to come straight away. We climbed down and tried to run to Matteo, but the drivers that had stopped kept us away. I could see a blood-stained coat covering his head, and by the time my dad got there, the police and ambulance had arrived on the scene, and the road was closed off.

The three of us were arrested. I was taken to a cell and sat there, unable to process what had just happened. Eventually, Dad was allowed into the station and did everything he could. After giving a statement, we were finally released, and he took me home. He never said a word, and for the first time in a long time, 'I felt safe.' He ran the shower for me. After I showered, he came into my room and lay on my bed beside me. He put his arm around me, kissed me and said, "My boy, my boy, I've got you, always." At that moment, I wanted to stay in his arms forever.

Now, I sit in this lobby, waiting to be called in. I look at him with his steel eyes, and he sits upright in his reassuring calm and wise manner and is in complete control, which amazes me.

I never realised, but for all these years of going to the cinema and pretending to be that guy on the screen, I was in fact living with a superhero all along, but I couldn't see it.

Proverbs 17-27

Whoever moderates his words is learned and prudent. And a man of learning has a precious spirit.

Why

Utterly and completely exhausted and bewildered; along with the unimaginable cold that was slicing into us like a carving knife. I had the feeling of breathing in serrated ice, cutting into my throat.

It felt like my brittle fingers would snap at any moment, as I struggled to open the instructions scribbled on the back of a cardboard cereal box. Eventually we reached the meeting point on the shore. I found the men in charge of the crossing and cautiously handed over our money; literally everything that we owned was now in their hands including our future.

The four of us huddled together trying to find some warmth, in an impossible situation. Our children in the centre so to conserve their body temperatures.

My wife remarked on how calm the sea looked; like a millpond, and how the bright moon was capturing our breaths as they rose up and disappeared into the crisp night sky.

Finally, the spluttering sound of a diesel outboard engine could be heard, before two men brought the boat around from the cove. Everyone in the group glanced at each other, but saying nothing; but the look of anxiety telling the story. The boat was an old outboard vessel that was more of a puncture repair kit than a boat. It was something that should have been scrapped twenty years ago.

Hannah looked towards me and said, "Papa, this doesn't feel right!"
I remember looking at her saying, "Don't worry Hannah, it will be fine, I will look after you."
"Can we go tomorrow on another boat; Please?"
I said, "Hannah, in six hours, it will all be worth it, trust me!"
She replied, "I'm scared."
Quietly I whispered, "I know." And I put my arms around her and gave her a cuddle.

My wife looked at me with concern, but what was I to do. I couldn't get my money back and I couldn't afford another boat.

Finally we were told to run down to the shore. We put or life vests on and I picked up Hannah and carried her so her feet would not get wet.

They asked the ages of the children, and I replied, "Abe is nine, and Hannah will be sixteen tomorrow."

"Okay get on board and sit together."

I placed Hannah on the boat and went back for Abe.

My wife picked up our bag, but she was stopped.

One of the men said, "No, you cannot take this."
She replied, "But these are our belongings."

He grabbed the bag and threw it to one side and said, "This isn't a flaming cruise ship! now get on the boat and stop complaining, or you can stay here. Your choice!"

I helped her on and we all sat huddled together in a line. My wife in front, then Abe, and then Hannah and finally me.

All of these families along with us in the same situation, with the same concerns and same fragile dreams.

My wife then looked back towards me and I smiled back, trying to hide my evident fear.

A man who was sat opposite me leant over and said, "Are you confident in this patchwork quilt of an excuse for a boat?'

"No I'm not" I replied.

Then he said, "Look at the two men in charge, and their new life jackets, now look at ours. If this boat goes down we don't stand a chance, I'm telling you! It will end in disaster!"

The engine started, and we pulled away from the shore.

As we did, other people appeared from the sand dunes and chased us down the beach and into the sea, shouting to us to wait, trying to catch the boat and to get a lift, but they were pushed back by the waves.

As we reached deeper water, I undid my trouser belt and slid it through the belt loop at the back of Hannah's jeans, and did it back up, so that we were secured together.

After an hour, Hannah said that Abe was falling asleep and her ribs were aching, and she was finding it hard to breathe.

By this time, it was past midnight, so I called out and said to everyone, "Its my daughter's birthday today, and she is sixteen." Everyone congratulated her and for a while we all smiled and felt alert.

Eventually though, the boat grew silent again, with only the engine roaring; like a lion charging its way through the waves.

Some time later on, the boat slowed down and called to six men in a yellow paddle boat.

The driver of our boat shouted out, "You're crazy, you will never make it, the wind is picking up."

They shouted back in a language I didn't understand, and we then carried on.

By now the sea began to crash against the boat; waves came up and over the side until I felt the sea coming up around my feet. As I looked down, the water was gradually filling the bottom of the boat and we were beginning to panic

The water was pushing the back of the boat down, so everyone rushed to the front. I couldn't move as Hannah was attached to me. The men in charge shouted to get back, or the boat will capsize; then that was it,......... We were in the sea. Everyone was screaming and as for the boat, starting from the rear it was going down. I scrambled with Hannah trying to swim away.
A flare went off lighting up the sky.
I struggled to stay afloat, and Hannah was no longer kicking!

I woke to the sound of voices calling to me.

I lay on the beach with the side of my face buried in the wet sand. I heard a man say, "Here; I found someone, a man attached to a girls body."

I cried out, "NO, no, no, no,……… No!"
Looking to my side, I saw Hannah and I pulled her closer to me and held her in my arms.

The man called somebody else on his phone and said that he had found two migrants, but the girl was deceased.

In a broken voice, I called out, "She is not a migrant,……..she's my daughter."

Meanwhile only twenty miles away, a surprise party was being held on a river boat cruise to celebrate the16th birthday for a girl called Lucy.

They moored the boat along the jetty. Everyone disembarked and walked down to the beach, where a barbecue had been organised, along with a live band who were playing.

Later in the evening her mother and father took Lucy to one side. Her father took out a diamond bracelet from his pocket which was engraved with her name.
Lucy offered her arm as he secured it around her wrist and kissed her on the cheek.
"Thank you father. This is the best night of my life."

Finally fireworks were let off to celebrate her birthday, and to finish a wonderful night.

Back on the shore, Hannah and I lay on the beach. The coastguard took a name tag out of his coat pocket and wrote down her name. I offered him her arm, and he strapped the tag around her wrist.

Then I kissed her on the cheek, and holding her tightly; I said "Goodnight sweetheart."

He bent down, put his hand on my shoulder, looked at me and said; "I am so truly sorry."

I looked back to him and said, "Am I the only one left?"

He replied, "Yes."

"How did this happen to them; how? I was trying to give them a future, not take it away!
Why?
Please; tell me why?
Because I don't understand!"

Matthew 5:5
Blessed are those who mourn, for they shall be consoled.

Sharvi

Bustling traffic, like bulls on the rampage in the chaos of the city that never sleeps.

Bikes, buses, cars, and people scurry in every possible direction in pure mayhem in the smoke-filled heat that takes your breath away.

Beggars and bankers on the same street corner. One trying to cross, whilst the other trying to survive. One with their dirty hands stretched out in a cry for help. The other, the other with his manicured hands firmly in his pockets.

A young crippled girl called Sharvi, pushes herself around on a skateboard for a wheelchair, a skateboard that was given to her as a gift. It was found in a rubbish heap and was ready to be thrown away, discarded as useless with no worth. A missionary sister who found it gave it to her, giving it and Sharvi a new lease of life. One leg crossed under her bum, and the other cut and bruised, being dragged from behind, rubbing it into the ground.

It was freedom and her opportunity to be independent.

She desperately looks up to people on the streets in need, though she is invisible to everyone who passes her by. She picks up thrown-away magazines advertising holidays and villas aboard, thinking, 'I would love to travel the world one day.'

During the never-ending rush hour, when trying to beg her way through another day, a car hits a motorbike, which crumples and careers off the side of the road and into the oblivious pedestrians.

Sharvi is hit and killed instantly.

The ambulance arrives. With little fuss, and as people wander by with their cameras at the ready, looking out of curiosity rather than concern, the paramedics open a zip bag and take her body away, like garbage being collected on refuge day. The pavement returns to normal, her blood quickly blends into the oil-filled tarmac, and within an hour Sharvi is not even a memory in this fast-moving city.

Within a few hours, a backpacker waiting for his bus notices the skateboard next to the pavement. He looks at it for a while and then realises that it has been abandoned, so he picks it up, brushes it off, and gets on the bus leaving the city.

For months he travels through different countries, taking his skateboard as his only full-time companion, recording and taking selfies of his journey and posting his blog along the way.

Eventually, along with a friend he met, he returns home to Milan. He offers the skateboard to his friend, who continues his journey throughout Europe until he also decides to return home.

When he arrives back in London, he uses his skateboard as his only mode of transport, taking it everywhere with him. One day, he rests it against a wall, and when he turns to get it, he sees some teenagers disappearing down the road on it.

It was gone!

One evening, while walking down the street, the teenagers spot a car and recognise the driver. One of them gets on the board and rolls down the hill to the traffic lights, and unnoticed, he slowly pulls up beside the driver and, without warning, shoots him straight through the head. They run off, and the board is thrown into a bush, once more discarded and left for rubbish.

Early the following morning, a youth worker spots the board in the bushes on his way to work. He stops, picks it up and takes it to the youth hostel.

On arrival, he calls the children into the yard and surprises them with their new present. He gets some water and a sponge, and they clean it. As they do so, they can see scraped into the wheel, the name 'Sharvi'.

James 4:14-15

Consider that you do not know what will be tomorrow. For what is your life? It is a mist that appears for a brief time, and afterwards will vanish away. So what you ought to say is: "If the Lord wills," or, "If we live," we will do this or that

Levende

Mouldy Bread

"Eat your food."
"I can't."
"EAT YOUR FOOD."
Sobbing, I said, "I can't! I don't like it."

Mummy slammed her fist on the table and said, "Eat your bloody food."
Now crying and snot dripping into my meal, I put my head down and start to eat.

Mummy stands by the kitchen window and lights a cigarette, her hand trembling as she offers the cigarette to her mouth.

"I'm sorry mummy."

I see her grinding her teeth, with tears cascading down her face as she looks away.

"Can I have some bread please?"
She opens the cupboard, takes out half a loaf, picks off the mould, and puts it in the toaster. She then puts jam on top to mask the stale taste.
"Thank you mummy," and she kisses me on the head.

The doorbell rings. I see the colour drain from her face, and her head drops as she sighs. She opens the door, and it's our landlord. He is a much older man who looks like a rat with grey skin, and he smells, and I don't like or trust him. He also goes to Granny's house to collect her rent and Granny hates him as well. Mummy starts whispering to him. I know she owes him money, and I also know we don't have any. Mummy lets him in and turns up the TV.

She tells me there's a problem with the window in the bedroom, and she wants to show the landlord. They go in and shut the door behind them. The problem is that she didn't turn up the volume on the TV enough.

I sit on the sofa, nibbling my toast whilst watching a cartoon, but I'm worried about her. I want to go in and protect her, but I'll sit here because she will get mad. After five minutes of eternity, they come out, and he says the window is jamming. "I will send someone to fix it for you." He stops, looks at me and then at my dinner; he then notices the countless ruined scratch cards on the table. Then he raises his eyes to mummy and tells her she is a disgrace, he puts his head down and walks out the door.

Mummy heads to the bathroom and I can hear the water running and mummy cleaning her teeth. I sneak into our bedroom, hoping the window is stuck, but I can open and close it easily.

I do my homework whilst mummy has a vodka and looks straight through the TV.

I look up and say, "I don't like our landlord."
"I don't either" Mummy replied.

I ask her if we can go to the park. I don't want to, but I want to cheer her up, and that's the only thing I can think of.

We leave home and go down the main graffiti-lined stairs because the lift smells of urine.

The stairs are littered with needles, and in the corner are a bunch of dead flowers to Daniel, who was found dead in the corner last week. His apartment is now boarded up along with several others.

Everyone is disappearing!

Outside we walk over to the playground avoiding the dog poo, and we sit on the swings with the stench of marijuana surrounding us.

I decide to push Mummy for a while and sing her a song. Eventually, I stop pushing her, give her a tiger bear hug, and then stroke and play with her hair.

She looks up and smiles, but her gaze falls back to the ground. I know she is broken, and there is nothing that I can do.

I'll have to be brave.

I wonder! She wouldn't be in this situation if I had never been born.

Is it my fault?

We go to bed, say our prayers and cuddle until she finally falls asleep.

I can feel the warmth of her skin and her breath on my forehead. I think we're protecting each other.

The following day, I let mummy rest in bed. I make breakfast with the leftover bread and scrape the last of the jam out of the jar.

I take a weed that looks like a flower off the kitchen window ledge, place it in a cup of water, and put it beside our bed. I give her the biggest squeeze and a thousand kisses. Then I go to school.

School is freedom, I don't feel trapped and I like my teachers.

At the end of the day, Miss Jenkins gives me three gold stars for excellent work. Excitedly, I rush home and up the stairs, along the corridor and towards our front door.

My face is beaming, 'Mummy will be so proud of me, we could go to the shop and buy some sweets!'

I stop and freeze!

The police are outside with my auntie, who is crying.

She;....... looks at me with her head tilted to one side.

I think to myself, 'My flower is dead'.

As I walk away with my auntie, I see our landlord coming out of another home, and he gives me a wink.
I don't understand.

Matthew 18:6

But whoever will have led astray one of these little ones, who trust in me, it would be better for him to have a great millstone hung around his neck, and to be submerged in the depths of the sea.

Levende

Shadows within the light

Dazzling neon lights burn into the summer's night sky. Beckoning people and drawing them into the narrow cobbled streets like flies to a trap; whilst the Devil himself, so full of pride and excitement, dances on the rooftops like a ringmaster weaving in and out of the shadows within the light.

Georgia hesitantly crosses the pavement and walks into the dull-lit lane nestled between the brightly lit shops. Filled with anxiety, she takes a deep breath and knocks on the paint-flaking solid metal graffitied door. She waits for an answer before finally being allowed in.

Greeted by a man, she makes a coffee and nervously lights a cigarette before heading towards the changing room, past the countless posters tacked to the walls that line the grubby fly-infested corridor. She calls her mum to ask if the children are in bed; her mum reassures her and tells her to calm down. Her mother asks if anyone else is helping her to clean the offices tonight.

"No, only me."

"Well, be careful. Love you sweetheart."

"I love you too Mum."

She takes a shower and then gets dressed. She puts on one stocking and then removes her prosthetic leg. Using a walking stick, she enters the front room, sits on a red heart-shaped sofa, and checks her reflection before pulling the cord that opens the curtain.

Showtime!

Looking out the window, she can see people wandering by, looking in and taking photos while laughing at her plying her newfound trade. Some young men bang on the window hurling abuse at her before staggering away.

Finally, a man knocks on the door, and she lets him in. They discuss the terms of business, to which he agrees, and with a heavy heart barely disguised by a smile, she closes the curtain.

She lays back, looks towards the ceiling and thinks to herself, 'My body is nothing more than a fetish freak show for someone else's sick pleasure. I am just something you paid for; now, all I can do is perform.

Lying there on her back, her throat stretched out with her head dangling off the edge of the sofa, and her hair falling softly on the blood-red carpet. Her tears run up her face and disappear into her fragranced brunette hair while trying to make sense of her reality.

She looks towards the drawer the girls call happy time! She feels the temptation to open it, but she doesn't want another excuse to fall back to where she came from, especially because of a deadly excuse called fentanyl.

Across the city, in a mansion, her auntie looks out of her bedroom window towards the neon lights before saying her prayers and going to sleep.

The following day, within the grounds of the mansion, a man is playing golf with friends on his perfectly manicured lawn, then hears a voice shout out, "Where are you?" he runs in the opposite direction hoping she doesn't spot him, while his friends laugh. She is a 4ft 9 Spanish 60-year-old nutcase who terrifies him, and she is also his housekeeper.

He has everything, which is hard to imagine. He started with nothing, and now he lives in a 21st-century mansion surrounded by acres of gardens and people who will not say no to him.

When he tiptoes through the polished marble hallway with his shoes on, she appears from nowhere, shouting at him to get off her floor, saying, "It's my house; now get outside." When he does something she disagrees with, she will look up and smile sarcastically and then say with her strong Spanish accent, "Jesus is watching you like a hawk, and there is not a shadow big enough for you to hide behind." He always laughs at her, and she smiles back, but underneath her smile, he knows she is deadly serious.

Sometimes, he would drop her off in the old town on a Sunday morning so she could go to Mass. He would often take a Ferrari or a Lamborghini, only to embarrass her, as he always has to pull her out of the car.

One morning, as he pulled up outside the church, Margretta held his hand and said, "Thank you for giving Georgia a job. Her mother and I have been so worried about her and the children. I hope her cleaning is as good as mine."

He replied, "I believe she is very good at her job, and the clients are all very impressed with her professionalism."

Margretta said, "That's good; she is a wonderful young woman; look after her."

Margretta was content with life. She enjoyed her work and felt part of the family, even though she knew her position.

Late one evening Margretta's sister called her in tears, to say that Georgia had been attacked at work and she had been taken to the hospital. Margretta stopped what she was doing and rushed to the hospital to be with Georgia.

On arriving, the police were there along with her sister. Her sister ran towards Margretta and punched her whilst frantically screaming and shouting. Margretta fell to the ground, unable to defend herself and not knowing what was happening. The police restrained her sister and explained to Margretta that Georgia had been attacked in a brothel where she was working. The Devil lay on the floor beside Margretta, mocking her and laughing in her face, calling her a fool.

"I don't understand. Why was she cleaning a brothel? She cleans offices for my boss."

The Devil laughed uncontrollably mimicking Margretta saying "I don't understand, I don't understand. UNDERSTAND THIS!

Georgia is mine and you cant do anything, because she allowed me into her life. UNDERSTAND NOW! NOW GET OUT!'

The police officer explained, "Georgia wasn't cleaning the property; she's working as a prostitute."

"No, No, No, you have this all wrong. My boss is a good man who employs her to clean."

She looked at the police officer, then looked at her sister before collapsing to the floor.

"What have I done? God forgive me."
"FORGIVE YOU!" Joked the Devil. "There's NO ONE to forgive you!"

Her sister looked at her and said she never wanted to see her again. Margretta picked herself up, walked out of the hospital, got into her car, and then broke down and cried.

Feeling alone, like she had never felt before, she returned to the mansion, walked in through the door, up the stairs and into the master bedroom where her boss and wife lay asleep and screamed at him. As Margretta unleashed her anger, his wife's face dropped in horror as the truth poured out. He jumped out of bed, dragged Margretta through the house by her hair.

The Devil shouted with excitement, "Yes, Yes, Yes."

Her boss then told her to collect her belongings and threw her out of the house, saying, "No one disrespects me, neither will you. Get out of my house; I do not want to see your face ever again."

She picked up her belongings put them into the car and drove away from the mansion. As she went down the driveway, she felt full of rage, anger, disbelief and confusion whilst the Devil waved and blew kisses at her through her car's rearview mirror, mocking her as she left.

She drove to her sister's house, but the door was slammed shut in her face, so for several nights she slept in the car until she decided to go to the brothel to find Georgia.

Knocking on the door; the same man answered. He explained that Georgia would not be returning. He could see the despair on Margretta's face and invited her in for a coffee. As they walked down to the kitchen, she noticed the posters that lined the walls.

Margretta said to the man, "These are all scripture quotations."
He smiled and replied, "Yes, they are."
"Why?" She asked.

He said, "My daughter used to work in a place like this and it killed her. She became an addict, and eventually overdosed. My wife died an alcoholic, as the pain of losing our daughter became too much for her to bear. This is where I feel I need to be, to look after these women the best I can. I can't control what they choose to do, but I am here to listen to them and try to look after them. I am so sorry about what happened to Georgia. It happened so quickly that there was nothing that I could do. Please forgive me."

Now the Devil smugly lays on the brothel rooftop, whilst the city and its hills burn all around him. He claps with excitement and glee, as he watches some young men injecting their arms full of death and sin.

He shouts out to the men, "I am coming to get you, and I will destroy you, you are mine!" before grimacing with a contorted face and squealing like a pig, as he is pulled back on his owners leash.

1 Peter 5:8-9

Be sober and vigilant. For your adversary, the devil, is like a roaring lion, traveling around and seeking those whom he might devour. Resist him by being strong in faith, being aware that the same passions afflict those who are your brothers in the world

Levende

Ryan Mcguire

Jumping down out of a garbage truck onto East 33rd Street. Ryan looks at his reflection in a window, adjusts his tie, and then, with an air of sophistication that he believes he is entitled to, he steps forward into a 'new' day.

Walking through Mid Manhattan with his head held high and eyes like steel, he feels like he is the King of New York; dressed in a $5000 suit and a $20,000 watch. He has such unbelievable confidence and a swagger to match; he honestly believes that he was born to be here. He stops to have his shoes shined and sits on an old office chair raised upon a wooden platform on the corner of the sidewalk. He watches all the people scurry on by and thinks, 'This is such a long way from Ireland, but this place fills my every ambition.'

As his shoes are being buffed, two teenage boys fight in front of where he is sitting. The man buffing Ryan's shoes 'shouts' at the teenagers and chases them off around the corner, but when the man returns, Ryan is nowhere to be seen.

Ryan walks past a lady carrying several bunches of flowers. One of the teenagers who was fighting picks a bunch out of her bag and makes his escape without the woman noticing that she has just been robbed.

Ryan continues walking towards an art gallery. As he confidently approaches the door, one of the teenagers passes him the 'freshly picked' flowers.

He looks into the window, admires his reflection, checks his hair, and then strides into the gallery.

He holds the flowers behind his back and smoothly walks up to a woman called Megan.

And in his strong Irish accent he says,
"Megan, I was just passing and saw a lady selling these roses, which made me think of you. 'So dinner tonight?'"

"Thank you Ryan, but I'm working."

"Surely tomorrow night then."

"Maybe!"

"I'll take that as a yes."

He smiles, and before she can reply, he turns and walks out the door, feeling assured of his impending success.

As he walks along he takes a pair of broken glasses, puts them in his breast pocket, and then makes his way with no urgency to the subway on 33rd Street. As he turns the corner to walk down the steps, a man coming up from the subway walks straight into him. Ryan falls back, pulls the glasses from his pocket and accuses the man of breaking his $1000 designer glasses. After some arguing, the man, who is clearly a tourist, admits fault for breaking the glasses, agrees to pay for the damage and gives Ryan $350. With cash in his pocket, Ryan decides that is enough work for the day, so he heads home.

On his way back, he collects his young son from school and chats to the parents in the playground. They all believe that he runs a successful business in the city. All the moms love him, and the dads think he is full of ….

Once at home, he makes his son do his homework and then the chores around the apartment. The two teenagers walk through the door and empty their pockets from their hard day of thieving. Ryan makes them all dinner, and then afterwards, he plays with the three boys before telling his son to have a shower before going to bed, but not forgetting his prayers.

The following morning, they all get up and after breakfast he takes his son to school. After kissing him on the forehead, Ryan tells him to stay out of trouble, and he watches him go off to the playground with his friends.

Ryan goes to the station and gets on a train heading for the city. As the train pulls into Pennsylvania Station, the two teenagers run through the carriage and push over a smartly dressed lady. Ryan helps her back up to her feet and ensures she is ok. After showing concern for the lady, he gets off the train and heads up to the street. There, one of the teenagers hands him a bracelet that they swiped from the woman.

He decides that it would be a good idea to get rid of the bracelet as soon as possible, and then, as the genius that he so 'obviously' is, he has a brainwave!

He takes it to a shop that his friend works in, he has it gift-wrapped and placed into a bag. He then heads to the Art Gallery and places the bag into Megan's hand.

"So, how about tonight? You can't possibly say no."

Megan opens the bag and can't believe her eyes.

"Ryan, It's beautiful, and as for tonight, Yes."

"I'll pick you up here at 8 pm."

He walks away and thinks to himself, 'You are punching way above your weight; don't mess this up you fool.'

For the rest of the day he cannot concentrate, just waiting for 8 pm. to arrive. In the afternoon he goes to St Patrick's Cathedral and lights a candle for his mother and his late wife Cathy. As he quietly sits in the corner the priest sees him, then comes over and sits beside Ryan and says,

"Ryan, Are you keeping out of trouble?"
"I'm trying to Father," he replies with a smile.
"And how about that son of yours and your nephews?"
And with a seriousness in his voice, he replies, "They are good thanks Father."
Then in a compassionate and loving fatherly way the priest quietly asks, "Have you told them about the cancer Ryan?'

"No Father, how do I? After what happened to Cathy, it will destroy them. They don't need to know; not now. Anyway, I'll be fine!"

"But Ryan!"

"No Father I cant."

"But who's looking after you Ryan?"

Ryan buries his head in to the palms of his hands and says "I dont know."

"Listen to me son! I am always here for you, understand?"

"Yeah, I know."

"Well, look after yourself Ryan and I want to see you at Mass on Sunday."

"OK Father."

After some time praying, Ryan gets up and goes back to the station and says to one of the teenagers, "Go and collect your cousin from school and take him home. Make a meal and make sure you all say your prayers before bedtime and tell him Daddy won't be back until late."

7:45 p.m. and Ryan heads back down to collect Megan from the Gallery. He nervously paces up and down, preparing himself, his palms sweating and anxious; for a man with such confidence, he appears completely out of his comfort zone. Then with a deep breath and pretending to be full of confidence, he walks towards the door, glances at his reflection and walks on in.

He sees Megan behind a counter; he walks up to her with his face beaming like a kid at Christmas. As he moves closer, he notices that she looks dejected; suddenly, a woman moves out from behind Megan and to his horror, it is the woman they mugged on the train. He instantly turns to walk out, but the security guards close the doors, and the police stand in front of him.

He realises that there is nothing that he can do, his shoulders slouch as he accepts his defeat, but he asks Megan, "How did you know?"

Megan replies, "This is my Mom, and this is her gallery; I would have gone out with you regardless of the bracelet."

Ryan thinks to himself, 'I almost struck gold; I was that close.'

He is taken away, but with his head held high because he doesn't want anyone to believe he is a nobody.

That night whilst being held in custody, he is allowed to call his son.

This is the hardest conversation because he loves him without question, and he wants his son to be the man he pretends to be, the man he so desperately wants to become.

He says goodnight to his son and is taken back to his cell. The door closes behind him, throwing away all of his dreams and naive ambition.

He sits on his bed, buries his head in his hands and thinks,

"I was that close!"

At his trial, Megan is called to testify. As she gives evidence, she is aware that if Ryan is sent to jail, his nephews will have to care for his son, or he will have to go into care. She thinks to herself, 'These boys are no more than children. How will they look after him?'

She looks over to her mom, looks at Ryan and then looks at his nephews. 'If I tell the truth, then his family will be torn apart; if I lie, my mother will not forgive me. What do I do?'

The lawyer asks her what happened, and she tells him the truth but does not elaborate, as she does not want the boys to lose his son.

At the end of the trial, he is given a six-month custodial sentence and taken away. As the teenagers leave the court, Megan watches them walk down the stairs. She looks at her mom and says, "I can't let this happen." She rushes down the stairs and around the corner.

Six months later, Ryan jumps down out of a garbage truck onto East 33rd Street; he looks at his reflection in a window, adjusts his tie, and then, with an air of sophistication that he believes he is entitled to, he steps forward into a 'new' day.

He walks into the gallery. Megan is standing behind a counter and smiles at him. Then Megan's mom walks towards him and says, "It is your first day, and you are late! I'm telling you now, If you mess this up which I am sure you will, I will make sure you regret it. Stay away from my daughter, put on your security badge and don't move away from the door."

Ryan looks at her and says, "Thank you Ma'am, you won't regret it," as he proudly puts his badge on, and gives Megan a wink.

Joel 2:12-13

Now, therefore, the Lord says: "Be converted to me with your whole heart, in fasting and weeping and mourning. And rend your hearts, and not your garments, and convert to the Lord your God. For he is gracious and merciful, patient and full of compassion, and steadfast despite ill will

I Thirst

Under the burnt red sun and the deadliest heat my brother was born.

A whisper he cried for a scream was more than he could muster. Our mother lovingly took him to her breast, but with tear-filled eyes for that was all she could do for him, but his mouth remained dry.

I would stare at him for hours, 'though I was lost of all expression,' just gazing into his tiny innocent face. As for me, my face was engraved with the agonising torment and pain of life. A gift from a famine that would surely be my death sentence.

But as for tears;   I have none.

I thirst!

I look towards my mother in my naive childlike desperate hope.

Her eyes completely vacant, lost in her devastation.

Grief is etched all over her face, revealing her anguish and pain rolled into one.

Flies gather all around like vultures, kissing me on my cut and broken lips.

My father; on his knees. His tears roll down his face and off the tip of his nose. He somehow summons the strength to dig a pit with his bare hands.

Why is he digging into the dusty ground?

My mother will not even look at me; no one acknowledges my existence.

I struggle with every breath I take.

"Father, don't cry, please.

Please, I beg you.

I'll be better soon, I promise. I just need to drink."

I will rest for a while.

I Thirst!

My lungs no longer able to summon another breath.

.

.

.

It's finished!

John 11:35

And Jesus wept.

Levende

In memory of Uncle Owen

Printed in Great Britain
by Amazon

59113260R00092